Averil supposed she ought to be thrilled at having been whisked out of obscurity to potential stardom on the stage, under the guidance of the celebrated director Philip Conway—but she wasn't. Already she had been foolish enough to fall in love with him—and even if she had any reason to believe he returned her feelings, what was she to do about her engagement to John?

LADY IN THE LIMELIGHT

BY

ELIZABETH ASHTON

MILLS & BOON LIMITED
17–19 FOLEY STREET
LONDON W1A 1DR

First published 1976
This edition 1976

© Elizabeth Ashton 1976

ISBN 0 263 71986 3

*Made and printed in Great Britain by
Richard Clay (The Chaucer Press), Ltd., Bungay, Suffolk*

CHAPTER ONE

THE poster in the shop window advertised the next performance to be given by the Thespian Amateur Dramatic Society during the week after Easter in the Lady Raydon Theatre at Elmsford, and below the details of dates and prices were printed the names of the principal actors and actresses taking part.

Two girls stood on the pavement studying it, the younger one being exceptionally pretty, with a milk-and-roses complexion and fair curling hair, although she had marred her youthful freshness with an excess of make-up. Her sister, the elder by some eighteen months, wore none and at first glance was unremarkable, though her dark expressive eyes under a broad low brow, straight nose and mobile lips held the promise of beauty, but her long brown hair, falling from a centre parting on either side of her face, obscured much of the delicate moulding of her cheeks and jaw.

'Doesn't it give you a thrill to see your name in print?' the younger girl asked. 'I'm so glad we've got nice names, Averil and Cecily Avon. Just think if we had an awful surname like Moggs!'

'I don't think it matters,' Averil remarked, 'you could always take a stage name if you weren't satisfied with your own. No, it doesn't give me a thrill to see my name plastered all over the village, even though it isn't Moggs. I love being in a play, but all that,' she waved her hand towards the poster, 'doesn't appeal to me at all. It's just a form of self-advertisement.'

'What's wrong with that?' Cecily demanded. 'You can't get anywhere without advertisement, self or otherwise.'

'But I don't want to get anywhere,' Averil objected. 'I'm happy where I am.'

'In this one-horse place?'

'Elmsford suits me, I'd hate to leave it.'

'You can keep it.' Cecily turned away with a discontented pout of her painted lips. She was a restless, ambitious creature, yearning for the bright lights of London, which was under fifty miles away, but since she was not yet eighteen, her parents had set their faces against a job in town. Later, they promised vaguely, pointing out that she would stand the chance of a better position if she stuck to her present one—she worked in a dress shop—until she had earned a good reference to back her applications. Cecily had agreed unwillingly to postpone her exodus, but she never ceased to grumble about the backwardness of Elmsford. This was a large village strung for nearly a mile along a secondary road between two country towns. It was famed for its old inn and its fine church. It also possessed Raydon Towers, a fine hall belonging to a family called Mortimer. Lady Raydon had been on the stage before she married Arthur Mortimer, the present holder of the title and the Towers. She had never lost her interest in her former profession, and she had instigated the Society to which the girls belonged and had built a miniature theatre in the grounds of the Towers to house their productions.

Averil had a deep and sincere love for acting. By it she could express her reserved personality, but unlike her sister, she was not an exhibitionist, and shrank from the acclaim which her efforts earned for her, for she possessed unusual talent, but was without ambition. The Thespians' bi-annual productions in which

6

she took part satisfied her needs, and she deeply venerated Lady Raydon who had devoted a great deal of time and trouble to developing her gift and instructing her in theatrical technique. They were fortunate to have that rapport between actress and director which can produce quite astonishing results.

Cecily was not in the same class as her sister, though her looks and her vivacity raised her above the average level, but she did not take kindly to correction and had had more than one brush with her producer.

'We're only doing it for fun,' she had argued, and complained to Averil that Lady Raydon was after all a back number and things had probably moved on since her day.

'Possibly,' Averil admitted, 'but the Thespians are lucky to have a director of her calibre, we owe her a lot.'

'Of course you think she's marvellous!'

Averil returned simply: 'I do.'

She worked as a typist in a solicitor's office and she was going out with a youth called John Woods. Theirs was a friendship dating from their schooldays and she expected in the course of time to become his wife. She envisaged no more exciting future than to obtain—with luck—a small house in the village or one of the nearby towns, easily accessible by bus, and spend her days caring for John and their children, with an occasional performance with the Thespians for diversion.

Cecily's contempt for country life extended to John.

'He's a drip,' she summed him up.

'He's nothing of the sort, he's a good, steady young man.' Averil became unusually heated. 'He's utterly reliable and will never cause me a moment's anxiety.'

'Nor give you a thrill either,' Cecily sneered.

'I don't want thrills, I'm not romantic.'

'No, you're just an old stick-in-the-mud, and he's

7

another, so I suppose you're suited, but this child intends to get a bit more out of life!'

Such remarks, and they were frequent, caused Averil to feel uneasy about her sister. She feared Cecily's discontent might lead her into some rash action. There was a strong streak of protectiveness in her love for her sister. Their parents had always been a little remote. Mrs Avon was a teacher and had gone back to work as soon as her children were old enough to start school. Her husband was a post office clerk, a quiet gentle man with a passion for stamp collecting. His daughters suspected his collection meant more to him than his family did. It had fallen to Averil's lot to mother her sister and condone with her manifold and vociferous woes. The bond between them was very close, their differences in temperament complementing each other. Even in the thorny matter of boy-friends they had not clashed. Cecily sampled all the available material and pronounced that it was composed of drips and wets and that no one exciting ever came to Elmsford. Averil never strayed from her John.

He did not aspire to act, but officiated as the Thespians' stage manager, and even the critical Lady Raydon admitted that he was efficient in that capacity. Thus he and Averil had a common interest, but she could not say he was exciting. She wondered vaguely what her sister meant by that word, and she distrusted thrills. The placid affection she felt for John was surely a good foundation for marriage, and more durable than any sudden infatuation. Actually their relationship was more fraternal than passionate; he had only ruffled the surface of her emotional potential, the depths of which were discernible in her acting, but she was quite unaware of this.

On the Saturday afternoon before the performances which would take place on the following Thursday,

Friday and Saturday nights, Averil had been invited up to the Towers for tea, and a final polishing of her part by her monitress. She always enjoyed these private sessions with Lady Raydon, and the beautiful drawing room with its luxurious furnishings appealed to a sensuous side of her nature, as yet undeveloped. The tall windows opening on to a terrace with their heavy silk curtains and vista of lawns and shrubberies satisfied her artistic eye, as the daintily served afternoon tea pleased her palate.

Lord Raydon was rarely at home; his hobby was zoology and in pursuit of it he was usually abroad searching for some rare animal. The two Mortimer boys were at boarding school, and their father was pleased that his wife should have found such an absorbing interest in her amateur theatre, it left him free to follow his own bent, and she managed his estate more competently than he did himself. Their romance had been brief, and both were content with their semi-separation. From time to time Lady Raydon had theatrical friends to stay, when she was alone, for she maintained a lively interest in her old world and dabbled in several stage ventures.

Averil walked up to the Towers through a showery spring day in March, for Easter was early that year. She wore a raincoat and head-scarf over trousers and tank top, as she was not expected to dress up. She turned in through the impressive gateway of the hall, where the lawns on either side were starred with daffodils and lilac bushes edged them, purple and white. The sky overhead was pale blue between voyaging masses of white cloud. A maid answered her ring— Lady Raydon possessed maids, but they were Italians —and took her coat and scarf from her. Averil ran a comb through her rich brown hair, falling as usual on either side of her face, straightened her white and green tank top over her green trousers, and followed the maid, Lucia, through the wide panelled hall to the drawing-room door.

Her hostess waved to her as she came in, and indicated a vast armchair opposite to her upholstered in blue brocade, into which Averil sank, her slight, boyish figure looking lost in its cushiony depths.

Georgina, Lady Raydon was a slim, elegant woman, with fair hair beautifully done and as yet untouched by grey. Her face was unlined, and still looked youthful, owing its preservation to intensive care with unguents and skilful make-up. The glowing youth of the girl opposite to her made her appear artificial, but Lady Raydon had no envy of her juvenile charms, only a faint regret for vanished years.

Between them was the tea table, laid with fragile china cups and saucers, thin curls of bread and butter, sandwiches and rich cake. Lucia appeared bearing a silver tea-pot, and Georgina proceeded to pour out, while she discussed the play they were about to put on.

'Of course it's a sentimental comedy,' she said, 'without much meat in it, and your part doesn't give you any opportunity to use your considerable emotional force. We must find you something more dramatic for next season.'

'I've no wish to show off,' Averil demurred, 'and I love the play we're doing. It may be sentimental, but it's charming, and the period costumes are so pretty. I'm sure it'll be a great success in the village.'

'I think so too, that's why I chose it. It's a nice antidote to the smutty rubbish we're deluged with nowadays.'

'My sister thinks it's insipid, and old-fashioned.'

'Cecily favours the avant-garde,' Lady Raydon said with an indulgent smile. 'But I don't think Elmsford

10

would appreciate modern sophistication. You're not much like Cecily, are you, dear?'

'Not a lot. Cecily complains that I've no ambition.'

'Haven't you?'

'No, and I'm glad. Ambition makes you discontented, doesn't it?'

Georgina looked at her curiously. A successful amateur actress usually dreams of professional triumphs, but this one seemed to have no inclination that way.

'Then you've no desire to try your wings? I mean, you've got considerable talent which might take you far.'

'I'd hate to have to go away,' Averil exclaimed vehemently. 'All I want, all I love is here, and as long as you'll have me in your plays, I'm perfectly happy.'

'Though you're only a big fish in a small pond?'

'Sounds horrid when you put it like that, but I don't care about bigger ponds. I just enjoy acting, and if it pleases the people who come to watch me, that's perfect.'

'You're easily satisfied,' Lady Raydon remarked drily.

Averil smiled beatifically. 'Isn't that fortunate? Poor Cecily gets so discontented, I'm glad I'm not like her.'

Lucia opened the door and announced:

'Mr. Conway, madam.'

To Averil's surprise this announcement threw her hostess into what could only be termed a flutter, she had never seen her smooth composure agitated before. Her hand flew to her immaculate coiffure, and she sprang to her feet with a flush upon her porcelain face, as a man came past the maid into the room. She went forward to meet him with both hands outstretched.

'Philip! I wasn't expecting you until this evening.'

He took her outstretched hands in both of his.

'Does that mean my early appearance is inconvenient?' he asked.

'You know your appearance is always welcome at any hour,' she returned warmly.

The newcomer raised each of her hands to his lips with a theatrical gesture. Averil watching him was aware of antipathy. He was too slick, too suave. His thick thatch of fair hair was cut short, and his lean brown face was faintly lined, especially about the mouth, which was thin-lipped and satirical. His eyes, a bright azure, were the coldest she had ever seen, with the hardness of blue ice. Above medium height, he had powerful shoulders tapering to a slim waist, and he moved with supple precision. He wore a black polo-necked sweater with grey trousers, the sable shade emphasising his fairness. Mechanically her mind registered:

Enter the blond beast.

But why such a thought should have occurred to her she could not conceive.

Georgina withdrew her hands, remembering Averil's presence.

'This is Philip Conway,' she introduced her friend, 'an old colleague of mine. Philip, meet our local bright star, Averil Avon.'

Philip Conway inclined his head. 'How do you do, Miss Avon. I gather from that remark that you adorn Gina's pet hobby, her amateur theatre.'

Lightly spoken but with a faint sneer, so that Averil gathered that Mr. Philip Conway was not impressed by amateur ventures.

Evidently Lady Raydon thought so too, for she told him:

'You needn't be so contemptuous of our efforts. We're much appreciated in the locality and we always get full houses, which is more than you can say!' She turned to Averil. 'Mr. Conway, as no doubt you know, is a theatre director of some fame.'

Averil did not know. She was familiar with the names of most of the current actors and actresses in the profession, but not with the directors and producers. Feeling that her presence was no longer desired, she stood up, saying:

'I must be going now, Lady Raydon.'

'Nonsense, you never leave so early. Don't let Philip's arrival drive you away.'

'Oh, but...' Averil was beginning feeling that Georgina's words could not be sincere, but Philip Conway cut short her protestations.

'Please sit down again, Miss Avon, or I'll never be able to forgive myself for intruding sooner than I was expected. You wouldn't want to make me feel uncomfortable, would you?'

There was a gleam of mockery in the narrow blue eyes. He knew quite well that it was not he who was feeling uncomfortable. Nevertheless, she did sit down again, not knowing how to insist upon departure. She was disappointed, for she had been looking forward to a cosy chat with her hostess. Now this man had had to come butting in precluding any more intimate talk. As soon as she could extricate herself gracefully she would be on her way.

Lady Raydon fussed over her new guest, of whom she evidently thought a great deal. She rang for fresh tea and seated him beside her on the sofa. Averil gathered he was staying for several days.

'I felt in need of a breath of country air,' he told them, 'if you can put up with me, Gina.'

'Need you ask? Stay as long as you like. Unfortunately the boys are due home for their Easter holidays, I hope they won't disturb you?'

'I don't suppose we'll get in each other's way,' he observed casually.

Lucia brought in the tea, and when he had been served with a cup, Georgina asked with genuine interest:

'What is your next production going to be, Philip?'

'*Romeo and Juliet.*'

'Oh no! It's been done to death.'

'I've never done it, and there's always a new generation coming up which hasn't seen it. It's a perennial favourite and I've always wanted to produce it. I can get a lease of the Regina in August so I'm going to put it on under my own direction. It's to be in modern dress, for after all the theme isn't all that dated, the rebellion of passionate youth against the tyranny of established prejudice and hate. The duel scene will be a modern brawl with Tybalt using a flick knife.'

Lady Raydon looked dubious. 'I don't know how that'll go down,' she said. 'I hope you won't lose a lot of money over it.'

'So do I. I gather you won't want to be included among the sponsors?'

'Oh, I always back you, Philip. Mad as your ideas often seem, you've a way of coming out on top.'

Lord Raydon had inherited a fortune from an American mother and he allowed his wife a free hand in its administration knowing she had a much shrewder business sense than he possessed. Lady Raydon frequently played fairy godmother to promising theatrical ventures and did not often lose by them.

'I have, haven't I?' Philip agreed with a complacency that caused Averil to deduce that he was either inordinately vain or overwhelmingly confident. Probably the latter, he did not look the type of man who would make an error of judgment, nor would have any pity for failures.

'How far have you got with resurrecting this hoary antique?' Lady Raydon asked.

'We're considering a suitable cast. I've tentatively approached——' He mentioned several well-known names. 'I want Nigel Forbes to play Romeo. He's a rising young actor.'

'He'll be excellent in the part,' Georgina approved. 'And the Juliet?'

'Ah, she's always difficult. She must be very young and at the same time have experience. It has been tried with a tyro, Italian I think she was, but...' He shrugged his shoulders expressively. 'Gemma Knowles might be a possibility.'

'Oh, no!' Georgina exclaimed vehemently. 'Not that little tart!'

Philip raised his eyebrows. 'She's no worse than the rest of her colleagues, and she has a kittenish charm.'

'A kittenish charm for Juliet! She couldn't play it, Philip.'

'She will when I've finished with her,' he returned with such grim relish that a shiver ran down Averil's spine. She could imagine him withering some unfortunate girl with cold cutting sarcasm, but then Gemma Knowles was very far from being a novice and must have learned to take that and worse.

'You're a bully, Philip,' Lady Raydon said, confirming Averil's assessment of him. 'I pity the poor little wretch, but surely that isn't the way to get the best out of a person?'

'What isn't? You know nothing about my methods, and Gemma and I may discover we're *en rapport*.'

There was deliberate malice in the last phrase and Averil caught a stricken look in Georgina's eyes. She supposed it was the knowledge that she was too old to play such parts herself, and Philip seemed to have the same idea, for he declared gallantly:

'Of course if you could be endowed with second youth, I'd have no need of Gemma.'

Lady Raydon smiled wistfully. 'A meaningless compliment since we can't put back the clock,' she said drily. 'Sometimes you're a bit of a brute, Philip.'

Philip shot a quizzical glance towards Averil.

'Please, Gina, not before the children.'

'Averil's no child, she's about the right age to play your Juliet,' Lady Raydon told him tartly. 'Gemma's too old.'

His blue gaze rested fleetingly upon Averil's flushed face, between the long strands of her hair, the simple styling, her immature figure and lack of make-up made her look like a schoolgirl, and she was not grateful for having his attention drawn to her.

'How old are you, Miss Avon?' he asked casually.

Startled, she told him, 'Nineteen.'

'As old as that?' He turned back to Lady Raydon. 'Juliet was supposed to be fourteen, but Italian girls mature earlier than English ones, so I suppose your protégée is about the right emotional age, but you see what I mean? Though the age may be right, youth alone can't compensate for gaucheness and inexperience. Most young aspirants can neither move nor speak properly.'

'Averil can do both,' Georgina declared.

'I beg your pardon, Miss Avon,' the glacial blue eyes appraised Averil with a mocking glint. 'I'm afraid I was very rude. I'd forgotten you've had the privilege of being trained by dear Gina, so you can be neither gauche nor raw.' But his tone indicated that Lady Raydon had not made a very good job of her. 'Are you doing anything now?'

'She's Phoebe in our production of *Quality Street* which comes off next week,' Lady Raydon told him.

'Good lord, whatever made you put on that sentimental mush,' he exclaimed.

'It has memories for me,' Georgina said archly, and he

looked faintly embarrassed. 'I'm sure the village will lap it up, besides which Barrie is a classic.'

'But won't your bucolic audience find it a bit dull? It isn't a play amateurs can perform adequately. That interminable first act!'

After which devastating remark and a disparaging glance towards Averil, he addressed himself to his tea.

Averil looked appealingly at Lady Raydon hoping that she would refute this sweeping statement, but Georgina did not seem disposed to take up the cudgels in defence of her company. Obviously she was pursuing another train of thought, for her eyes held a mischievous sparkle as if some idea for disconcerting her guest had occurred to her. But Averil had had enough of him for one afternoon and devoutly hoped she would never encounter him again, so she made another attempt to depart.

'I really must be going, Lady Raydon...'

'Just a minute, Averil,' Georgina bade her. 'I would like Philip to hear you read something before you leave.'

Surprise and consternation showed in both her companions' faces. Philip ejaculated rudely, 'Oh lord!' while Averil exclaimed, 'I couldn't possibly.'

But Lady Raydon had been challenged, her perception and her competence called into question. She was aware that Philip had been unfavourably impressed by Averil, and wanted to vindicate her interest in the girl, and justify her championship of her. That Averil would be caused acute embarrassment did not seem to have occurred to her. She walked to a bookcase that contained various sets of plays, and drew out two copies. Returning, she handed one to Averil, and drawing up a stool sat down beside her, announcing:

'Act Two, Scene Five.'

Averil saw that she was holding a copy of *Romeo*

and Juliet. Mechanically obeying the voice of authority, she leafed through it to find the required scene, then she paused and raised beseeching eyes to her hostess's face.

'Please, Lady Raydon, Mr. Conway can't possibly want to hear me ... us ... read anything, let alone this play.'

Philip was regarding them both with satirical amusement.

'It's no good, Miss Avon,' he told her. 'I know Gina of old. Once she's made up her mind there's no stopping her. Better go ahead and show me your paces, which I fancy is the object of the exercise.'

He settled himself on the deep sofa in an attitude of resigned patience, half closing his eyes. Averil noticed, in spite of her perturbation, that his long lashes were dark brown instead of sandy as would be expected with his fair hair. A quiver of resentment ran through her. He need not be so openly contemptuous and it was not her fault that she was being forced to face this ordeal. He could have stopped Georgina if he had wished to do so, but he had no desire to spare her and afterwards he would ridicule her. She did not blame Lady Raydon for her predicament, for she surmised that she was as incensed as she was by Philip's attitude. Her diffidence was suddenly swamped by a wave of antagonism. She would show this insolent director that though she might not be up to his standards, she was not wholly incompetent, and she did at least know how to speak.

'Well, if I must, I must,' she said resignedly, and turned to the book.

It was a short scene between Juliet and the nurse when the lovelorn girl is waiting for the ancient retainer to tell her what Romeo has arranged about their marriage. Averil stumbled a little through the opening speech, painfully aware that the lines upon Philip's face were becoming more deeply etched with increasing derision. She longed for him to bid her cease and say he had heard quite enough, but he did not; perhaps she was lulling him into slumber, for the fringed eyelids wholly concealed his eyes.

With the entrance of the nurse, her nervousness vanished. So often had she gone over lines with Georgina that her familiar voice awoke an automatic response. She forgot her sardonic audience and became the ardent eager girl seeking the news that was so important to her.

'Sweet, sweet, sweet nurse, tell me, what says my love?'

Gradually Philip's eyelids lifted and he was looking straight at her, but Averil lost in her reading did not notice. She finished with her triumphant exit line and closed the book.

Raising her eyes, she met the intent stare of the blue ones opposite to her and quickly turned her head away, aware that she had blushed.

At least she had succeeded in waking him up and she anticipated that he might, just might, offer some sort of apology for misjudging her, but what he did say was entirely unexpected.

'I would like to hear you read the potion scene.'

A glitter of triumph showed in Lady Raydon's eyes, and she announced dramatically:

'Act Four, Scene Three.'

'I don't need the book, I know it by heart,' Averil told her.

The soliloquy in which Juliet makes up her mind to take the drug supplied by Friar Lawrence is a dramatic recitation for an aspiring actress, but Averil had never done it in public. The drama of the lines had appealed to her and she had memorised them and

19

acted them alone for the sheer pleasure that speaking them had given to her.

Georgina gave her the cue, and she began. Low-voiced but with increasing intensity, she spoke the famous words. Not using undue emphasis but with underlying emotional force, fully restrained, she expressed her terror of waking in the vault and the horrors that would surround her. Yet she never really raised her voice except when she called to Tybalt's ghost to stay. Finally she made pretence of drinking the draught, with courageous acceptance.

'Romeo, I come, this do I drink to thee.'

Sinking back in the armchair, she closed her eyes, feeling as exhausted as if she had run a marathon. From what seemed to be a long distance away she heard Philip's voice.

'I suppose that's an example of your direction, Gina, you must have worked very hard upon her.'

And Lady Raydon's reply.

'My dear man, I've done no such thing! I didn't know she knew any Shakespeare, and I've never heard her do it before.'

Averil opened her eyes and saw a blaze of excitement on Philip Conway's face, but it faded so quickly, to be replaced by his habitual sardonic smile, that she thought she must have fancied it. Although she did not realise it, he had set a deliberate trap for her with that speech, expecting a ham rendering. Nineteen out of twenty inexperienced young actresses would have ranted the so dramatic lines or been overcome by excessive emotion, but Averil's performance had been beautifully controlled.

Georgina said wickedly: 'Gauche and raw.'

If she had expected to disconcert him, she was disappointed, for Philip remained remote and cool.

'Thank you, my dear young lady, for a most interesting performance,' he told Averil. 'You have a musical and expressive voice and you do credit to your teacher.'

Which of course was what Lady Raydon wanted to hear, since Averil was her pupil. Averil experienced a faint sense of anticlimax. She had not expected anything more from him, she doubted if he ever praised anyone. Georgina had exhibited her like a performing puppet to vindicate her own efforts in Elmsford, there was no more to it than that. Yet she had reached such sublime heights in her acting, she had anticipated ... what?

Don't be a fool, she admonished herself. Thank God I didn't break down or dry up. Lady Raydon's pleased and I've wiped that condescending look off his face. What more could I possibly achieve? Naturally I can't compare with his Gemma Knowles.

Nor did she want to do so, she had never wished to become a professional.

'I wonder if after all that I might have a whisky and soda?' Philip asked, regarding his cooling tea distastefully. 'I feel the need of a restorative.'

'Of course,' Lady Raydon pressed the bell. 'Did my protégée produce such a devastating effect?'

'You are always full of surprises,' he murmured gently, but the look he gave her was anything but gentle.

Feeling dismissed, Averil stood up.

'Well, I'm glad I gave satisfaction,' she said a little tartly. 'And now I really must go. John was coming round this evening and it's getting late.'

'John?' Philip snapped, giving her a keen glance.

'The boy-friend,' Lady Raydon explained. 'Yes, run along, my dear, and thank you very much for being so co-operative. You've convinced Philip—Mr. Conway—that we amateurs have something to offer to our audiences.'

She threw a barbed glance at the director, and went to give her order to Lucia who was hovering in the doorway.

'I stand corrected,' Philip said to her back. He rose to his feet and bowed to Averil with pretence humility. 'Thank you, young lady, for opening my eyes to your great potential.'

A somewhat ambiguous remark, but Averil ignored it. She did not want any bouquets from him and she mistrusted the glint in his eyes, suspecting mockery. Ignoring him, she addressed her hostess.

'I'd gladly do anything for you, Lady Raydon, and I always enjoy acting. Goodbye. Good evening, Mr. Conway.'

His hateful voice pursued her.

'Give my regards to John and tell him he's got a treasure which I hope he appreciates.'

Averil hurried through the hall, her fists clenched, passing Lucia carrying the drinks tray, thinking she had never met a more supercilious and arrogant creature, and she hoped fervently that he would keep out of the way during the final rehearsals of *Quality Street*. Probably he would only stay for the weekend, she could not imagine there was anything in Elmsford that could attract such an obvious man about town. Meanwhile she would not mention his presence at home. Cecily would read all sorts of improbabilities into what had happened, and the last thing she wanted was to have anything more to do with Mr. Philip Conway.

CHAPTER TWO

THE church at Elmsford was decorated with the bounty of spring for Easter Sunday. Averil went to the early service, so missed the sight of the Towers party in the family pew at Matins. The boys were home, having arrived the previous evening after spending a few days with a relative.

'Had she any guests with her?' Averil asked, referring to Lady Raydon, hoping Philip might have been called back to London. Mrs. Avon said not, but probably he was not a churchgoer.

Although it was a holiday, Averil had promised to go up to the Towers in the afternoon to rehearse with the boys. They had been deputed to take part in the schoolroom scene in the play, their roles only comprising a few lines, which could easily be acquired in four days.

At the gates Averil met the young man who was playing opposite to her, and registered surprise, for he had said he had an engagement.

'So you've made it after all?'

'I didn't feel well enough to go to Bury as I'd intended, so I thought I might as well come along. Lady Raydon said she wouldn't keep us long.'

'Oh dear, Alf, I hope you're not going to be ill. Nobody'd manage to learn your words in time, in fact we haven't anyone who could play your part,' Averil told him anxiously.

'Oh, I'll be all right,' Alf declared, but as they

walked up to the house, Averil noticed that he was coughing a lot.

'It's only a bit of a cold,' he insisted. 'It'll probably be gone by Thursday.'

Because there would be only a few of them, they were not going down to the theatre, and as they left their coats in the hall, the third person called, Molly Smith, arrived. She was playing Avril's elder sister in the play. Lucia ushered them into the dining room, a vast apartment which had been cleared for their requirements, the polished table pushed to one side, and the chairs stacked upon each other. This room held some evidence of its master's travels; there was a zebra skin decorating one wall, and African gourds and weapons hung incongruously among the oil paintings in their heavy gilt frames.

The two Mortimer boys were waiting to receive them. Robert, thirteen years old, was a well-grown lad, his voice already beginning to break. Paul, three years younger, was a mischievous imp.

They greeted the visitors politely, but as Robert saw Averil was alone, his face clouded.

'Isn't your sister coming?' he asked.

'No, she wasn't called.' Averil was surprised. 'Your bit's not with her.'

Paul giggled. 'Bet he's sore about that. Bob's gone on her,' he explained.

'Shut your trap!' his brother growled, turning brick red.

'Says she's a dish,' the irrepressible one continued, 'and he wouldn't be in the play if it wasn't for her.'

Robert aimed a blow at his head, as Lady Raydon came into the room.

'Boys, boys!' she admonished, as Paul rushed towards her, crying: 'Bob hit me!' 'Where are your manners?' She sighed. 'Your father's no need to go looking for rare apes in Africa, he's got a pair here.'

Averil looked curiously at Robert's sulky face. He was starting young, she thought, but after all he was only four years younger than Cecily, and she had had an eye for boys as soon as she entered her teens, but she would not notice one as young as Robert, even if he were the future Lord Raydon.

'Put the chairs in the right positions, please, Alf,' Georgina commanded. She was wearing a smart Paris gown, and was looking beautifully groomed. As she usually attended rehearsals in slacks, Averil concluded that Mr. Conway was still at the Towers.

'You know it's a bit tough expecting us to give up our time to your rotten play when it's our holidays,' Paul complained.

'Don't be rude,' his mother rebuked him sharply. 'It'll do you more good than sitting with your nose glued to the television, which seems to be your favourite occupation.'

'Okay, Baroness,' Paul said cheekily, for so he addressed Lady Raydon when he wanted to annoy her.

Ignoring him, she suggested they made a start, but Molly, who had been hopefully watching the door, enquired:

'Is Mr. Conway still here? They say in the village he's a famous producer and I thought he might be going to give us a few tips.'

Averil's heart sank; the last thing she wanted was to be coached by Philip, and she looked apprehensively at Georgina.

'Mr. Conway is here for a holiday,' Lady Raydon said repressively, 'and I shouldn't dream of bothering him with our play. Nor do you need any tips, as you put it, from him.'

'I'd say not,' Paul chirped up. 'He'd make you howl. He's famous for making his leading ladies cry, isn't he,

Baroness? Besides, he isn't interested in *us*.'

Averil saw Alf and Molly exchange glances.

'Dreadful child,' Georgina sighed, thinking her sons were becoming too much for her; they needed their father's guidance, but Arthur was so ineffectual. 'Come along, we're wasting everybody's time.'

Averil was anxious to start; she had left John at home, he always came to tea during holidays, and she wanted to get back to him. She went over the short scene with Paul half a dozen times, a scene in which he told her she was ridiculed among his friends because she did not use her cane hard enough.

'She'd got the right idea,' he whispered to Averil. 'Nowadays we consider caning barbaric.'

'Barbaric or not, it's what you'll get if you don't keep quiet,' his mother said ferociously, having overheard him.

'Aw, Baroness, have a heart,' her offspring exclaimed. 'But you couldn't bring yourself to do it. You shouldn't threaten what you daren't perform.' His eyes sparkled impudently.

'Then I'll send you to Mr. Conway, he'd have no compunction about it,' Lady Raydon told him sharply, and Paul subsided.

'Lord no, not that creep,' he muttered.

'What did you say?' Georgina's eyes glittered dangerously, and Averil hastily intervened.

'Come on, Robert, let's do our bit,' she said urgently. 'I can't stop much longer.'

Robert only had a very brief appearance as the big boy who chases Phoebe with her own cane, before she is rescued by the timely intervention of Captain Brown. He considered the part was beneath his dignity and was sulky under his mother's admonishments. Averil was relieved when the uncomfortable session ended.

'Full rehearsal tomorrow on stage,' Lady Raydon

reminded them. 'Dress rehearsal on Wednesday. Alf, take care of yourself, you've got a nasty cough. Robert, show them out. Goodnight.'

This was an unusually abrupt dismissal, and Averil felt a little hurt. The boys escorted the three of them to the front door, Robert with grown-up dignity, Paul grinning wickedly.

'You must excuse the Baroness,' he told them. 'She's in a hurry to get back to her fancy man.'

'Don't say that!' Robert was shocked. 'Wherever did you pick up such a horrible expression?'

'Heard it in the village,' Paul said airily.

'Please ignore him,' Robert besought them. 'He doesn't know what he's talking about.'

'Holy terror, that kid,' Alf remarked as they walked away from the Towers. 'They ought to gag him.'

'There isn't really any gossip about Lady Raydon and—er—her friends?' Averil asked anxiously, jealous for her benefactress's good name. By friends she meant in particular Philip Conway.

Molly said primly, 'There's always talk when a woman's separated from her man. Why doesn't Lord Raydon come home more often?'

There was no answer to that. Months later Averil was to remember that conversation and all its implications.

On the Tuesday night Alf could barely get through his part, and on the day of the dress rehearsal he was in bed with bronchitis and forbidden to get up.

A forlorn and disappointed Averil came up to the Towers when she had finished work, having learned the disastrous news at lunch time. She foresaw that all their efforts would be wasted. The Thespians could not rise to understudies and she did not see what even the resourceful Lady Raydon could do to save the play short of reading the part herself, and that would be ludicrous.

Lady Raydon herself opened the door to her, and laughed when she saw her woebegone face.

'It's all right, child, you needn't look as if the heavens have fallen. Philip is still here and he'll play it.'

'Oh, no!' Averil exclaimed involuntarily, as she followed Georgina into the drawing room where to her dismay she saw Philip lolling on the sofa holding the text of the play.

'Why ever not?' Lady Raydon demanded. 'It's a marvellous bit of luck that he happened to be here, and what's more, he has played Valentine Brown.'

'In the far-off days of my youth,' Philip informed her, uncoiling from the sofa, and standing up to greet her. 'You see, I was an actor before I took to directing. Gina was in the same company and she was my Phoebe.'

'Couldn't she be it again?' Averil blurted out, revolting from the intimacy with this man which playing a love story with him would inevitably entail.

Lady Raydon laughed. 'I'm a bit past it, my dear,' she said deprecatingly. She looked severely at the girl. 'You should be very grateful to Mr. Conway for stepping into the breach.'

Averil flushed. 'Of course,' she murmured.

'You needn't be,' Philip told her. 'I only yielded under coercion, a threat that if I didn't help you out the Towers would be barred to me for ever and a beautiful friendship would be broken.' He threw Georgina a quizzical glance. His eyes returned to Averil with a slightly puzzled expression, for he was unable to account for her reluctance. 'Perhaps you consider I'm too old for the part,' he hazarded, 'but I'm told there's no alternative and of course the play must go on, so in those circumstances I must ask you to put up with me.'

'It isn't that,' Averil said honestly. 'But ... but ...

28

you'll find us so incompetent.'

'And gauche and raw? You'll never forgive me for that, will you?'

'You'll show us all up.'

'Philip will play down to you,' Lady Raydon said stiffly. 'He won't try to steal the show, if that's what you're afraid of.'

She was vexed by Averil's lack of enthusiasm.

'I never thought of that,' Averil declared in distress. 'Will he ... are you coming to the dress rehearsal to-night?'

Philip laughed. 'Naturally, I'll need all the practice I can get, in fact I may have to ask you to put in some extra time with me, if we can arrange it between now and tomorrow night.'

'I ... I'll do all I can to help,' she faltered.

He laughed again. 'I really believe you think I'm an ogre about to devour you, instead of,' his eyes glinted, 'make love to you.' He was eyeing her curiously, for her hair had been carefully curled into the ringlets necessary for the part, and she had pinned it up under a scarf, thus revealing more of her face and neck than was usually apparent. Though she had no idea of it, he was thinking that she was better looking than he had first thought possible.

'There aren't any love scenes,' she said hastily.

'Not exactly passionate ones,' he conceded, 'but the whole theme's a romantic love story, isn't it?'

She dropped her eyes, disturbed by his expression, though she did not suspect what was motivating it.

'I ... yes, I suppose so.'

'Good lord, girl,' he exclaimed impatiently, 'don't you know what the play's about?'

'Of course I do,' she returned with more spirit, 'but I can't see you as a Valentine Brown.'

'Ah, but you've never seen me act. I daresay we'll

surprise each other.'

And that, she thought, was quite possible.

Lady Raydon had built her own theatre in the grounds of the Towers, economically comprised of a Nissen hut raised upon breeze-blocks to give it height. The erection had been a battle with the local builder, she insisting that the dressing-room accommodation must be on a level with the stage, and he being imbued with the idea that a platform must always be approached by steps. The theatre had moveable seats and a good floor and could be hired out for other functions when the Thespians were not using it.

Averil, who had watched it being constructed, had a deep affection for it. She felt that she belonged to it, and it was a magic place where she realised all her dreams. Cecily spoke of it with contempt, describing it as a tinpot little place. She had only a small part in the play, for most of the characters were older women, and her first consideration was to be able to look glamorous. She was not jealous of her sister's greater talent and did not resent her having the leading part, until she met Philip. Ready dressed, she had been watching the first act, in which she did not appear, at the dress rehearsal. She came rushing into the dressing room which she shared with Averil where her sister was changing for her next scene.

'My dear, he's simply gorgeous! Why didn't you tell me? Aren't you thrilled to bits to be acting with him? You are lucky!'

The dress of the period showed off Philip's graceful figure, and he had augmented his hair with sideburns, make-up smoothing his face into the contours of youth. Averil had been painfully nervous when he had come on stage, but found him so responsive to act with that she quickly regained her confidence, and had almost forgotten who he really was.

'He's a lot better than poor old Alf,' she said sedately, 'which makes it a lot easier for me, but as a man he doesn't appeal to me at all.'

Cecily gaped. 'Sometimes I think you're crazy! I wish I was playing Phoebe.'

Averil laughed. 'You know you'd hate to have to learn so many lines.'

Her own appearance was transformed, though she had had some difficulty in curling her hair into the ringlets that are described in the play, and the high-waisted Empire dress displayed unsuspected feminine curves, but for the second act, which is dated some ten years later, when Phoebe has become a schoolmistress, a grey gown and cap eclipsed her, as they were meant to do.

'Shame you've got to make yourself such a guy,' Cecily observed, touching up her make-up in the mirror and eyeing her own (natural) yellow curls complacently. 'But you soon blossom again in the ball dress.' She swung round and looked at her sister through narrowed eyes. 'This is a wonderful opportunity for you, Avvy.'

'I don't get you.'

'To make an impression upon him, of course.'

'I've already done that,' Averil told her, moving towards the door. She smiled mischievously. 'He thinks I'm gauche.'

Philip had put in some intensive work with Georgina before the rehearsal, familiarising himself with the stage and the moves, and the words were coming back to him. When he did dry he disguised it very cleverly. In the second act, when Captain Brown, as he is then, returns from the wars, he wore uniform; luckily the one hired for Alf fitted him, and looked exceedingly handsome. The stir in Averil's pulses when she beheld him was not altogether acting. It was strange to see ardour in his eyes instead of the familiar mockery and she had to remind herself that he also was acting.

Since she had no change of costume for the ballroom scene, being already arrayed in the very becoming white satin gown she had donned in the previous act, she was waiting backstage while the set was changed, and John came up to her.

'You're surpassing yourself tonight, darling,' he told her. 'Our new acquisition seems to inspire you, and I must say he's a great improvement upon Alfred.'

'He wouldn't have to be very great to be that,' she said, laughing, for Alf was very much an amateur. 'He's awfully easy to act with.'

'So it seems, but don't go and fall for him,' John admonished, with a flash of jealousy.

'How could I when I've fallen for you?'

'I'm such an ordinary guy,' John said with false modesty, for he had his share of masculine vanity and wanted to hear her contradict him.

'And I'm only an ordinary girl,' she declared, disappointing him.

'I'm not sure you are. There's something about you that makes me afraid you'll fly away from me one day.'

She stroked his cheek. 'I've nowhere to fly to, and my place is here with you.'

Someone called for John, demanding to know where he had got to.

'I must go, my minions need me,' he observed. 'Carry on the good work, darling.' He put his arm about her and made to kiss her cheek.

'Be careful,' she warned, 'this hair-do takes ages to arrange.'

'I claim that privilege for the run of the play,' a voice announced behind them, and Averil turned swiftly to confront Philip, spectacular in his tight breeches, frogged tunic and shiny boots.

'You're the stage manager, aren't you?' he went on, addressing John. 'Shouldn't you be overseeing the setting of the scene?'

'I'm on my way,' John said stiffly. 'And in case you don't know it, Averil's my girl.'

'Pro tem?' Philip suggested suavely.

'For all time,' Averil corrected him.

Again John was called, and he hurried away reluctantly.

'So you're a believer in love eternal?' Philip enquired scornfully.

'That sounds pretentious,' Averil strove to speak lightly. 'But ... well, yes, I can't imagine I could ever care for anyone except John.'

'One does imagine that sort of thing in one's teens.' Philip addressed the corridor above her head. 'At forty the perspective has altered.'

'Are you really forty, Mr. Conway?' Averil asked, surprised, for he seemed too vigorous to belong to her parents' generation.

'Not quite,' he told her, subtly flattered, 'but I've reached an age when I've become cynical about so-called love.'

'Then you're not married?'

'God forbid!'

Since she was a girl who liked to think well of everyone, a reason for his cynicism occurred to her.

'Perhaps you were crossed in love when you were young and that's why you feel as you do,' she remarked sympathetically. 'Was there some barrier between you and the girl you wanted?'

A shadow crossed his face as if she had flicked a raw spot, then his mouth twisted sardonically.

'The women I've wanted were willing enough without matrimony,' he told her brutally.

He was revenging himself for her naïve suppositions,

33

and possibly he intended to shock her. The wide, candid eyes gazing up at him were disconcerting. But she did not recoil as he had expected. Instead she said gently:

'Poor Mr. Conway, you must have been hurt at some time or other and you've let yourself become warped. If only you knew it, you're missing so much by becoming embittered.'

The sincerity in her voice robbed the words of any suggestion of impertinence.

'Well, really, I never expected to be lectured by a romantic teenager!' he exclaimed, half amused, half annoyed by her perspicacity, for there had been a painful episode in his youth.

'I didn't mean to lecture you, and even teenagers know something of life, especially nowadays,' she pointed out. 'But being so happy myself, I want everyone else to be the same.'

'That's a tall order,' he returned, and lightly flicked her cheek. 'My love life has been vastly different from your innocent romance.' His eyes narrowed and he looked at her penetratingly. 'I don't think you've any idea of your possibilities. You've only scratched the surface of your emotions.'

'Whatever I've done it satisfies me,' she told him quietly.

'And you but ... what was it? Nineteen?'

'Are you implying that I'll change?'

'Of course you will. You haven't grown up yet.'

'I'm as grown up as I'll ever be,' she insisted, with a vague uncertainty beginning to disquiet her. Before this man's worldly sophistication she was indeed a child, and was it possible she might become discontented with her life? 'I couldn't be disloyal ...' she was beginning, seeking to reassure herself, when a stentorian voice shouted:

'Beginners for Act Three!'

Several people came out of the dressing rooms, among them Cecily, resplendent in a ball gown and looking extremely pretty.

'Ah, Philip,' she exclaimed coyly, running up to him. 'I may call you that? Stage people don't stand on ceremony, do they? You look quite magnificent, poor Alf's bronchitis is our gain.'

'You're most flattering,' Philip murmured insincerely, his eyes resting contemptuously on her pretty, pert face and yellow curls. 'But the stage is waiting.'

Cecily never lacked confidence and she tucked her arm into his as they proceeded stagewards in Averil's wake.

'I wish I were playing Phoebe,' she said with a sigh. 'Averil doesn't appreciate her luck.'

'She may learn to do so,' he said cryptically as they reached the stage.

Dress rehearsals are notoriously trying whether professional or amateur, and this one was no exception. There were hitches, lights that fused, and the motley collection of village folk recruited for the ball scene were more willing than talented. The act limped along until the final scene between Captain Brown and Phoebe. In this the play reached a different plane. Averil responded brilliantly to Philip's expertise. Masquerading as her niece, her charming coquetry changed to incredulous disbelief, then passionate repudiation as, covered with shame, she realises he is revolted by her antics as Livvy, and it is her normal quiet, lady-like self he really loves and she has spoilt it all by her behaviour.

Standing in the wings, after his exit, Philip said to Lady Raydon who had joined him:

'That girl has the makings of a great actress.'

There were, as Philip had remarked, no passionate

love scenes, only in the final one does the hero kiss the heroine, and Averil by then had so thoroughly identified herself with her part that Philip had become the character he was playing, and throughout the three performances of the play she continued to do so. The real man became submerged in the personality of her stage lover, and when she met him backstage, he would pause to smile and touch her cheek, or with skilful fingers rearrange a curl that had become displaced, his actions seeming entirely natural. Even when waiting in the wings he laid a proprietorial arm about her shoulders she did not resent it. It was not until the last evening at the supper given after the performance to the cast by Lady Raydon that she suddenly realised the fantasy was over, that on the morrow he would be returning to London and she would most probably never see him again. She was alarmed and dismayed by the sense of desolation the thought brought to her.

Lady Raydon discouraged the presentation of bouquets after the final performance, declaring that the practice promoted envy unless everyone received one, which was absurd, but during the last act someone put a bunch of carnations in the Avon girls' dressing room.

'Those look like products from the Raydon hothouses,' Cecily remarked, pouncing upon them, as they came in after the final curtain call. 'From Philip, I bet.'

But when she looked at the card attached, her complacency was drowned in dismay. 'Miss Cecily Avon from an admirer,' she read out, 'and the initials, R.M. Avvy, what do I do? He's only a schoolboy.'

'You don't do anything,' Averil told her, 'except say thank you. But do it discreetly, he may have pinched them when the gardener wasn't looking.'

'Highly probable, I'll just wear one to show him I

appreciate the gesture,' Cecily said, detaching a blossom. 'But what would his mother say if she knew?'

'Nothing, she'd only smile indulgently at his precosity, and he'll be going back to school. After all,' Averil's eyes became dreamy, 'John and I started when we were his age. He used to pull my hair, but he always mended my bicycle punctures.'

'You may have been a child, but John was nearly sixteen and as mature as he'll ever be.'

Averil refused to be ruffled. 'I was thrilled—my first boy, and my last.'

It did not seem very long ago, but a gap seemed to be opening between the present and her schooldays, She hurriedly began to remove her make-up. John would be waiting for her and she wanted to compensate him for the neglect necessitated by her absorption in the play. Normally he understood that, and she had no need to feel guilty, if her absorption had been only in the play. Had it?

'I can't see Robert pulling my hair,' Cecily said, giggling. 'He's a sweet kid. Makes me feel as if I were sitting on a pedestal.'

Averil smiled wryly. Calf love, crushes, youthful infatuations were all part of growing up and could be quite painful. She recalled that Philip considered she herself was still immature. Was she juvenile enough to have a crush on him? If she had, the circumstances had been unusual, so perhaps it was excusable. The image he had presented to her was not his true self, but a romantic figure created by the play. The real Philip Conway was a supercilious, sarcastic creature whom she had not liked, and now she had returned from the realms of makebelieve to everyday life, he could be no danger to the genuine and abiding affection she had for John. In actual fact they were as far apart as Cecily and Lord Raydon's son.

'Different worlds,' she said aloud.

'What?'

'Nothing, just thinking. Are you ready, Cis?'

Together they left the dressing room, leaving the red and white carnations hurriedly thrust in a basin, an offering to love's first pangs.

The supper was a buffet meal laid out in the auditorium after the audience had gone, and was as informal as were the clothes of its participants. Several of the girls including Molly Smith had dressed up in long dresses, but most of the men wore trousers and sweaters. Robert smiled shyly at Cecily and came hurrying to attend to her wants. Paul was engaged in stuffing himself with the delicacies his mother had provided. Lady Raydon, regal-looking in dark green velvet with a string of pearls, watched over the proceedings like a benign goddess, directing her Italian handmaidens to ensure that everyone's wants were receiving attention. John immediately monopolised Averil, leading her into a corner, where he had arranged chairs and a small table. He was feeling it was time that he asserted his prerogatives. He had not been blind to the notice Philip had taken of her. There was nothing he could put his finger upon, free and easy camaraderie was usual in a theatre, but some instinct was warning him that their relationship was threatened.

The party was well under way when Philip appeared. He had been up to the Towers to change and was wearing a lounge suit which even Averil's inexperienced eye could see was beautifully cut; it looked quite different from the one John wore on Sundays. He had bathed and shaved and without the sideburns and make-up to which she had become accustomed he looked an unfamiliar stranger. There was a flutter among the female members of the cast as he came in, and Molly Smith, who had had several scenes with him in the play, ogled him invitingly, but Lady Raydon indicated a seat beside her at the top of the long table, and beckoned to Lucia to bring him refreshment.

Involuntarily Averil found her eyes straying towards him, and she had difficulty in responding to John's trite remarks, which she often did not even hear. For four days she had been in close contact with the enigmatical personality across the room, and had fallen under his spell. Now he had gone back to his own sphere, and she was merely a simple village girl to whom he would have nothing to say.

'I don't believe you're listening to me,' John complained. 'Where've you gone to, Avvy? I asked you the same question twice.'

'Sorry, John.' She smiled at him wanly. 'I'm so tired. These have been a hectic few days.'

'Well, it's all over now,' John pointed out, adding viciously: 'And a darned good thing too.'

She looked at him in surprise. 'I'm always sorry when a production's over and there won't be another until next autumn. Didn't you enjoy it?'

'No,' he told her glumly. Then seeing from her expression that some explanation was necessary, he went on: 'It seemed different with a stranger butting in.'

'It wouldn't have gone half so well with poor Alf,' she pointed out.

'Perhaps not, but Conway's not one of us,' John said. 'This is our village theatre and we're all villagers.'

'Really, John, you should be grateful to Mr. Conway for helping us out of a jam. You sound jealous of him.'

He looked at her darkly. 'Perhaps I am.'

'That's absurd! You were never jealous of Alf.'

'No need to be. He didn't change you like this fellow has.'

'But I'm not changed, John,' she cried in consternation. 'And tomorrow he'll have gone away and *Quality Street* will quickly be forgotten. Everything will be as it always was.'

'I hope so.'

'I know so.'

Yet even as she said the words her heart misgave her. Was John right and she had changed? But that was impossible. She looked towards Philip and met his gaze. He smiled and she smiled back again. Then his eyes went to John and his lips curled in the familiar sardonic twist. Averil was sure that he had guessed the younger man's resentment and was amused by it. Something in the arrogant poise of his head, the quiet confidence of his attitude irritated her. Did he imagine he could take her from John with a flick of his finger if he were so inclined? She said vehemently:

'I'm not sure I even like him.'

'Like who?'

'Mr. Conway, of course. He was lovely to act with, but I'm sure he was secretly despising us all.'

John checked the protest on his lips. If she believed that so much the better, but he had noticed Philip's expression when he had watched Averil on stage and he certainly had not been despising her.

Averil knew that in her anxiety to pacify John she had not spoken the truth. She did not dislike Philip, but liking was hardly the right word to describe her feelings towards him. It was too anaemic, for he was definitely disturbing. She remembered that he had said he could obtain any woman he wanted for the asking, or so she had interpreted his cynical remark. She had pitied him, intuitively divining that his attitude was vengeance upon her sex for some past hurt, but she also divined that as a lover he would be very difficult to resist. Those subtle little advances throughout the show had indicated that he was always aware of her womanhood, even though she was immature. Even Lady Raydon was not impervious to his charm. Charm? She would not describe him as a charming man, he was too sarcastic, but he possessed an intangible something that could turn a woman on.

Abandoning her unprofitable reflections, for her association with Philip Conway was now a thing of the past, she turned back to John, who was eyeing her anxiously. It did not matter what Philip had or what he was, he was outside her orbit and John was her dear friend.

To round off the evening, champagne was served, an extravagant innovation which caused the guests to open their eyes very wide. Later it transpired it was a gift from their leading man. Lady Raydon rose to propose a toast to their saviour, for if Philip had refused to help them out there would have been no performance. The cast responded with enthusiasm, they gave Philip three cheers, and the champagne elevating them above their usual phlegm, regaled him with a rousing chorus of, 'For he's a jolly good fellow'. Jolly, Averil thought, was hardly descriptive of Philip, but that did not lessen her gratitude. Philip took it all in good part, making a few complimentary remarks when he could make himself heard, but there was no warmth in either face or voice and Averil suspected he was heartily bored by the ovation, an attitude that roused her ire. Though they might be country folk their feelings were genuine, which she felt sure was more than were most of the plaudits of his more sophisticated peers.

The time came to break up and it was then that, excited by the champagne, Cecily excelled herself. Most of the company had asked for Philip's autograph, which he wrote upon hastily acquired programmes, and now as they started to take their leave, she flung

41

her arms round Philip's neck and kissed him soundly. Though he looked slightly taken aback, he rose to the occasion, returning her embrace. That touched off the other girls, who, led by Molly, crowded round him eager to give and receive a salute, which he obligingly permitted. Averil hung back shyly, for she had no wish to be publicly kissed, especially with John beside her, but as the excited girls ebbed away, she knew she must say goodbye. There were only a few people left as she approached him where he stood beside Lady Raydon, who had watched the scene impatiently, her arched brows raised above her grey eyes.

'Silly little idiots,' she was saying. 'You shouldn't have given them champagne, Philip, it went to their heads.'

'There's no harm done,' he returned, brushing powder off the shoulder of his suit. 'It's flattering that they don't regard me as an old has-been.'

Averil held out her hand. Wearing a plain straight dress, her hair, the ringlets coming uncurled a dark mass around her pale face, now innocent of make-up, she looked younger than her nineteen years, and a little frail.

'Goodbye, Mr. Gonway,' she said formally. 'Thank you for an unforgettable experience.'

She would have moved on, but he held her fingers firmly.

'Don't I rate a kiss?' he asked with a sly gleam in his eyes.

She was aware that John beside her had stiffened.

'I think a handshake between friends is more sincere,' she returned demurely.

'Do you need to play Phoebe Throssel in real life?' he enquired. 'Your colleagues have a more up-to-date approach.'

John intervened coldly. 'Averil is very tired, Mr.

Conway. I'm waiting to take her home.'

Philip gave him an insolent glance.

'That being so, my car is available to convey her. I don't think you possess one.'

'Oh, I'm not too exhausted to walk,' Averil protested, trying to free her hand, which Philip still held. 'It's not far and I'd like a breath of air.'

She sensed the rising tension between the two men and did not fancy the role of bone of contention. She was sure Philip was only teasing John, but the lack of a car was a sore point with him. He was saving hard to buy one so he could take her out in it. He was quick-tempered and she dreaded what he might say if Philip provoked him further.

But the director seemed to lose interest in them. A bored look crossed his face, as he relinquished Averil's hand.

'Goodnight,' he said abruptly, and turned away to speak to Lady Raydon.

'Thinks himself Lord God Almighty,' John complained as they went out of the theatre. 'I'm glad we've seen the last of him.'

Averil said nothing. Glancing over her shoulder, she could see through the open doorway Philip's illuminated figure as he offered his arm to Lady Raydon preparatory to escorting her across the gardens to the Towers. Both were laughing. At us, Averil thought resentfully, for the company had not shown up very well. In her simplicity she supposed Philip was used to more dignified society. Her fingers still tingled where he had gripped them. If John had not been there would she have kissed him? She knew what his lips would be like against her cheek, for she had been familiar with them in the play, but that had been makebelieve and she had not needed to return his kiss. It would be different kissing Philip Conway when he

43

was not portraying Captain Brown, and he would not have been content with merely her cheek.

John linked his arm through hers as they came out into the village street. All about them was the spring night and the scent of lilac, a first quarter moon setting behind the black bulk of the Towers.

'You're very quiet, sweetheart.'

Averil came out of her reflections with a start, guiltily conscious that her thoughts had been involved with embracing another man. Defensively she pleaded that she really was tired.

'Lucky it's Sunday tomorrow, so you can have a rest,' he remarked prosaically.

'I'm not sure it isn't Sunday already,' she said, for the street lights had gone out. 'Will you be coming to tea?'

'But of course, I always do.'

Suddenly the prospect of Sunday and all the coming Sundays seemed tame and flat—going to morning service, helping get the dinner, a walk with John and home again for tea. She was consumed with a new restlessness, a desire for she was not sure what. When they reached her door she was unresponsive to John's kiss which was never very exciting, for he did not consider it was correct to be too demonstrative before marriage.

As she crept up the narrow stairs of the semi-detached villa where the Avons lived, careful not to disturb her sleeping parents, the traitor thought occurred to her that John never would be very exciting; she even doubted if he were capable of deep feeling. Up to now she had been content with his placid wooing, secretly a little relieved that they ran no risk of becoming mired in the bogs of passion. Actually John seemed to regard passion as something not quite respectable.

44

Cecily was already asleep in the room they shared, having been given a lift home earlier on. Averil crept into bed in the dark, glad to conceal her flushed cheeks, for the thought had occurred to her that her future would be very different if she were to marry someone like Philip Conway.

CHAPTER THREE

NEXT day both girls were suffering reaction from the excitement of the previous week, and the inevitable flatness now the play was over. Cecily was peevish and complaining. Elmsford was duller than the proverbial ditchwater and Averil was a fool.

'Why so?' Averil asked blankly as she prepared herself to accompany her mother to church, while her sister lounged half dressed on her bed. She hoped the service would bring back to her the contentment she seemed to have lost.

'There you were in intimate contact with a man who is connected with various theatres and directs his own company. Yet you hadn't the nous to ask him for a part.'

Averil turned from the mirror by the aid of which she was endeavouring to pin up her hair under the little fur cap she was going to wear for church and stared at her sister.

'I never dreamed of doing such a thing.'

'Why not, may I ask? You're as good as heaps of professional actresses and it was obvious he admired you...'

'I'm sure he didn't.'

'Avvy, how can you be such a blind goose?' Cecily demanded.

'I'm sure you're mistaken,' Averil insisted, 'and in any case I don't want to go on the professional stage, there's too much competition.'

'You know nothing about it,' her sister returned, 'and it's against nature that anyone who can act like you can shouldn't want to make it your life's work. If only I'd got your talent, with my looks, I'd reach the sky. I've a good mind to go up to the Towers and offer our services to that snooty director.'

'Cis, you wouldn't dare!'

'There's no harm in asking, he could but say no, and he was rather sweet last night.' She touched her mouth reminiscently and giggled. 'Gave as good as he got!'

Averil found this reminder of Cecily's boldness a little distasteful. Naturally Philip had taken advantage of it, but she revolted from kisses that meant nothing, it was making oneself cheap.

'Well, you're too late, he'll have gone,' she said drearily.

'I'm not so sure about that.'

'He only prolonged his stay to help out with the play.'

'I wonder why he agreed to do that.'

'He wouldn't want to let Lady Raydon down.'

Cecily gave her sister a thoughtful look. 'Philip Conway doesn't strike me as the boy scout type,' she observed. 'Depend upon it, he had some selfish reason for being so obliging.'

'You always attribute base motives to everybody,' Averil told her accusingly.

'And I find I'm generally right.'

A melodious clamour broke the Sunday morning

quiet, and Averil grabbed her prayer book, exclaiming:

'The bells! We'll be late.' She glanced at her sister. 'I'll pray that you may be granted more Christian charity,' and she ran out of the room. Cecily's derisive laughter pursued her. She rarely went to church, and Averil knew very well that Cecily regarded her as a goody-goody. She did not mind, she only wished her sister could find some stable influence to guide her.

Mrs Avon was waiting for her in the diminutive hall and they went out together. They had not far to go. The Avons' house was only a few yards down a side street off the main road, and their way lay across the village green which sloped upwards to the church at the top. The main road ran past the Towers on their right, on the left a secondary road ascended the hill fringing the green with some nice properties abutting on to it. The church was a fine fifteenth-century wool church, but it had lost its original tower in a fire and the new one did not match its noble proportions.

They reached the church door as the organ swelled to greet the entrance of the choir, and crept to their seats unobtrusively. Thus it was that in the flurry of their near late arrival and the effort to compose herself suitably for her surroundings, it was a little time before Averil noticed the occupants of the Raydon pew. Georgina in short fur jacket and smart hat was accompanied by her well scrubbed offspring and, to Averil's surprise, Philip Conway.

She had convinced herself that he would be on his way to London and she would never have expected to see him in church. Yet there he was and acting the role of a devout member of the congregation, and that was precisely what he must be doing, for she could not believe his piety was genuine. Then she rebuked herself for her uncharitable surmise, for she was being as bad as Cecily, only she could not quite reconcile the Philip she knew with the very saintly-looking gentleman in the Raydons' pew. He looked so angelic, he only needed a halo to proclaim him a saint, and that was what made her suspect he was putting on an act.

He never once glanced in her direction, though the Raydon pew was an ancient boxed affair, set sideways to the aisle, and his profile was within her range throughout the service, to which she was soon paying scant attention. A pillar behind him threw it into high relief, and the light from a stained glass window turned his complexion to ivory and found glints of gold in his fair hair. Thus she had ample opportunity to study his face. His nose was possibly a little too long for perfection, and the haughty curve of his nostrils was responsible for his occasional supercilious air; the chin was square and cleft, no nonsense there, the mouth a little too thin-lipped to be handsome. It could be the face of a saint or a libertine and the dividing line was thin.

The congregation waited respectfully for the party from the Towers to precede them out of church. Both boys smiled at Averil as they went past, and Georgina faintly inclined her head, but Philip stalked down the aisle without a glance to left or right.

As they gained the porch, Mrs. Avon said:

'That was the man you acted with, wasn't it? I must say he looked a bit stuck up.'

'He isn't really,' Averil defended Philip, 'but I don't suppose he noticed us.'

They walked out into the bright spring sunshine, for it was a lovely morning. The trees surrounding the Towers and in the woods behind the church were uncurling their tender green leaves, the gardens of the houses bordering the green were full of blossoming bulbs.

Mrs. Avon looked about her appreciatively.

'All things bright and beautiful,' she murmured.

As they reached the church gate, Philip Conway stepped forward to intercept them, the Raydon family having gone on ahead, for he was alone.

'Good morning, Miss Avon,' he said genially. 'Quite recovered from last night's revelry, I see.'

'Oh, I'm fine,' she stammered, momentarily thrown off balance by his unexpected appearance. Hastily she recovered herself. 'I didn't know you were a church-goer.'

'Why should you? There are a lot of things about me you don't know.' He glanced at Mrs. Avon. 'Aren't you going to introduce me?'

'Oh, I'm sorry.' Averil feared he must be thinking she was being more than usually gauche. 'This is my mother—Mr. Conway.'

Mrs. Avon held out her hand and Philip obligingly shook it.

'We came on the first night,' she told him. 'It was lovely.'

'Thank you.' He glanced round. 'The dragon doesn't go to church with you, Averil?'

'The ... the dragon?'

'Or should I say Saint George? I rather fancy he cast me for the dragon.'

'Oh, you mean John,' Averil exclaimed, flushing. 'No, I'm afraid he doesn't.'

'He considers you don't need guarding in sacred precincts?'

Averil drew herself up very straight and squarely met the mocking blue eyes.

'You're not to make fun of my John,' she reproved him. 'I'll not stand for it.'

Mrs. Avon, though completely fogged, sensed something was amiss, and said placatingly:

'John Woods is a good, steady boy, even if he doesn't go to church.'

'I'm not denying it,' Philip told her. 'He's everything I'm not, and since you're alone, Averil, do you think he would object if we went for a stroll together?'

'Of course he wouldn't,' Averil snapped, stung by this suggestion of pettiness on John's part. 'But why?'

'It's such a pleasant morning,' Philip purred.

Averil glanced at him doubtfully. The discovery that he was still in Elmsford, the way he had accosted them had confused her, but she resented his sneers at John and could only imagine he wanted her to go for a walk with him to further annoy the other man, who would be sure to be informed of the incident by the village gossips.

'I'm sorry, but I have to help Mother get dinner,' she told him primly.

'Oh, that's all right,' Mrs. Avon declared obtusely. 'I can manage, you go along, dearie, a brisk walk would do you good. She's looking peaky, isn't she, Mr.— er—— Too many late nights, but I must say I enjoyed the play. It beats me how you could remember all those words—so clever of you.'

'It was, wasn't it?' Philip agreed with a perfectly straight face. 'Come along, Miss Avon—Averil, you've had your mother's blessing and I've something I wish to say to you.'

He drew her arm through his, and gave Mrs Avon his most devastating smile.

'Don't be late for dinner, Avvy,' Mrs Avon cautioned her, adding doubtfully, 'Perhaps Mr.—er— would like to join us?'

'Thank you, but with your permission I'll give Averil some lunch. I don't think I'll have time to say all I want to say before your dinner time.'

'I don't see what you can have to say to me,' Averil

said uneasily, trying to withdraw her arm, but he held it clamped to his side.

'Don't you want to find out?' he asked insinuatingly.

'I suppose it's some sort of theatrical business,' Mrs. Avon said vaguely. 'I must be getting on Mr—er—— Take care of Avvy, and don't be late for tea, dearie, you know John'll be coming.'

'Avvy,' Philip muttered under his breath, as Mrs. Avon ambled away. 'How do you stand for it? A pretty name like Averil mutilated!'

'Families always do call each other funny names,' Averil explained. 'But you're being a bit high-handed, Mr. Conway. I'm not sure that I want to have lunch with you.'

'Of course you do,' he returned, guiding her away from the church. 'Isn't your feminine curiosity burning to know what I have to say to you?'

'Not particularly. Curiosity isn't one of my failings.'

She had a premonition that what he was going to tell her would be disturbing, even embarrassing, and would be better left unheard.

'Then you're a most unusual young woman, but then we all know that.'

'You needn't jeer at me,' she said reproachfully. 'I know I'm naïve and ignorant, only a country girl, but I'm not ashamed of it.'

'Why should you be? You're altogether charming, Averil, so refreshing after the shameless hussies who inhabit my world.'

She still suspected he was laughing at her simplicity, but even if he were joking she felt a thrill when he called her charming.

He halted her beside a big maroon car and opened the passenger door.

'Hop in, little one.'

She drew back. 'I thought we were going for a walk.'

He made a face. 'Why walk when one owns a car? A car can go further afield. The suggestion of a stroll was merely a feeler, and since I've ascertained that dear John is out of the way until—er—tea time, we've all the afternoon before us.'

'You're taking too much for granted,' she told him with a quiver in her voice. One half of her very much wanted to go with him, but prudence was whispering that she should not do so. She did not wholly trust him and already she had been disloyal to John in her thoughts regarding him.

'I'd be grateful if you'd let me go home,' she went on. 'I . . . I don't feel any good can come of any further contact between us.'

'You don't do you, you stupid little idiot,' he said tersely. 'But although I find your prudishness irritating, I'm not going to abandon you. So kindly get into the car.'

Still she hesitated, and he enquired with steel in his voice:

'Must I abduct you forcibly?'

'You . . . you wouldn't dare!'

He was holding her arm in an iron grip and at her remark, his lips curled back in a smile that was almost a snarl.

'Try me,' he challenged her.

Averil capitulated. Out of the tail of her eye, she could see passers-by throwing curious looks in their direction. What would they say if they saw Philip push her into his car, for she did not doubt he meant what he said. His rudeness assured her that his intentions were not amorous, and perhaps she should at least listen to whatever proposition he wanted to put to her since he seemed to consider it so important.

'Very well,' she agreed. 'Since you're so insistent,' and she entered the car. Once seated, she rubbed the arm he had gripped so hard with a sidelong glance at him as he got in beside her.

'Sorry if I hurt you,' he said perfunctorily as he started the engine.

'You don't care in the least,' she accused him.

'I hate people who won't do what they want to do out of pure contumacy.'

'But I never pretended I wanted to come!'

The car bounced off the grass on to the road, as he asked:

'Can you honestly say that you didn't want to?'

She did not reply to that question; in her heart of hearts she knew that she wanted to go with him where-ever he led, and that this morning's meeting had been a reprieve from the desolation that had threatened to engulf her, but she dared not acknowledge the impli-cation of these dangerous yearnings, had not as yet re-alised their significance. Instead she enquired:

'I suppose you're never troubled by a tiresome con-science?'

'No, never,' he answered promptly, as he turned the car into the eastward road. 'Oh, I don't mean I don't know what's right and what's wrong, but if one has a supreme object in life it's foolish not to go all out for it without worrying about those who stand in one's way.'

'You sound a bit . . . ruthless,' she said faintly, feeling slightly repelled.

He shrugged his shoulders. 'That's one way of put-ting it.'

He halted two villages further on at an old-fash-ioned hotel in a tiny square. Here was a wealth of old oak beams, with copper and brass adorning white-washed walls and the ancient chimney breast. It was correspondingly expensive. Averil was glad that she was wearing her churchgoing clothes, a navy dress trimmed with white, a tweed coat with a black fur collar and her furry cap, under which her pinned-up hair framed her face showing the delicate lines of neck and throat.

Throughout the meal, which was not very exciting, but well cooked—soup, chicken and vegetables, followed by fruit pie and cream, Philip exerted himself to play the courteous host, which meant that he was at his charming best. He talked about the various productions he had directed, describing actors and actresses whom Averil knew by name and had seen upon television, amusingly and a little cruelly. She listened wide-eyed, glimpsing a glamorous world that was new and yet from her own experience not entirely unfamiliar. The jargon used by both the amateur and professional stages was much the same.

'Was Lady Raydon a great actress?' she asked during a pause in his reminiscences. They had been served with coffee and he waited to light a cigarette while he considered his reply.

'No,' he said finally. 'She was competent, but there was always something lacking. Of course she always looked gorgeous.'

'She said she appeared with you in the Barrie play.'

'That was when we were both very young and it was only a third-rate company. It was my first good part, but she was more experienced, she's some years older than I, you know, but she wasn't a good Phoebe.'

He was looking beyond her with clouded eyes at some vision of the past, his face falling into harsh lines. Averil sensed the memories he was recalling were not entirely pleasant ones. 'But I gave up acting in favour of direction,' he said after a pause, 'and she ... married.' He stubbed out his cigarette with vicious energy.

'She preferred love to her career,' Averil mused dreamily.

Philip flashed a scornful look at her pensive face, his eyes were hard and glittering.

'Oh yes, love,' he gibed, 'plus a title and a fortune.'

Averil's loyalty was instantly up in arms. Not content with mocking herself and John, he was now jeering at her adored Lady Raydon.

'I know Lady Raydon could never be mercenary,' she declared.

'You know nothing about it,' he snapped rudely. 'Wait until you're offered wealth and position even with a slob like Arthur Mortimer thrown in. Then if you refuse them you can talk.'

Her candid dark eyes met his hard blue gaze wonderingly.

'I'll never be offered anything like that, but if I were, I couldn't marry a man I didn't love. Didn't she love Lord Raydon?'

'Naturally she said she did,' he returned shortly. 'But it was difficult to believe her.' He laughed suddenly and the harshness left his face. 'But what can a kid like you know of the follies of men and women? You're still wrapped in your adolescent dreams.'

'I find them very pleasant even if they are dreams,' she returned, refusing to be ruffled. 'I can see you've become disillusioned, but with luck I'll keep my illusions until I'm middle-aged.'

'Assisted by the impeccable John?'

'Please, Mr. Conway, you've been so nice, don't spoil it all by making cracks about John. You know I don't like it.'

To her surprise he looked faintly ashamed.

'Sorry, little one, perhaps it's a case of sour grapes. I am disillusioned, as you say, and I've no right to try to dispel yours. But it's time we turned to practical matters. When do you expect to marry the admirable John?'

'Not for ages,' she said, her mobile face growing wistful. 'You see, we've got to save such a lot, we'll need a mortgage for the house and all sorts of things, and John wants a car.'

'Good lord!' he exploded. 'Do you have to contribute to all this?'

'But of course, why shouldn't I? Isn't marriage a partnership? I can't expect John to provide everything.' She sighed. 'Unfortunately I don't earn very much, and I have to give Mummy something towards my keep, so I'm afraid it'll be a long time before we can get married.' She looked at him apologetically. 'I'm sorry, I didn't mean to bore you with all that, it just slipped out.'

'I'm not bored, but very interested. You're just incredible.'

Her artless revelations seemed to be having a peculiar effect upon Philip. He was studying her through narrowed lids as if she were some rare specimen he had come upon by accident, and the smile edging his lips was both pitying and triumphant. She said defensively, for she was wishing she had not been quite so frank about her circumstances:

'I suppose most of the girls you have to do with are all gold-diggers.'

Philip's smile broadened at her ingenuous question.

'Most of them,' he admitted, 'or else they're absorbed in boosting their egos. When I said you were refreshing it was an understatement—you're like a crystal pool in an arid desert. But what you've told me makes the proposition I was going to put to you a lot easier.'

He paused to light another cigarette, while Averil waited in uneasy expectancy. As he seemed in no hurry to resume, she suggested:

'Is it some sort of job?'

'Yes.' He blew a smoke ring. Watching it ascend, he enquired, 'How would you like to be able to earn much bigger money and—er—' he made a grimace, 'by doing so speed up your wedding?'

Something to do with the theatre, she thought, and asked anxiously: 'But should I have to leave Elmsford?'

'I'm afraid so, but surely you can trust John to wait?'

'Of course I can,' she returned confidently, 'but I'd hate to have to leave home.'

Philip bit back a sharp comment. If he wanted to have his way with her he must exercise tact and understanding. She was sensitive enough to divine his underlying impatience and said apologetically:

'I know I'm an awful stick-in-the-mud, Cecily is always saying so, but it's the way I'm made.'

'But, good lord, girl, you've got exceptional talent. Haven't you any urge to use it?'

'But I do use it with the Thespians.' She looked at him eagerly. 'Do you really think I'm good? I thought I only seemed so because there was so little competition.'

'What a modest violet!' he exclaimed derisively. Then seeing her pained look, he went on more gently; 'I assure you you could hold your own with much cleverer players than those in your village drama group, and under my direction ... What's the matter?' For she had flinched.

Averil had remembered what he had said about Gemma Knowles, and his ruthless expression which had chilled her. She could hardly tell him that the thought of being directed by him terrified her, so she said evasively:

'Lady Raydon is a very considerate producer, she makes allowances.'

'Meaning I'm not and I wouldn't?' He grinned impishly. 'I aim to get results. But you needn't be afraid of me, my child, I'd be very gentle with *you*.'

She looked at him uncertainly.

'What are you getting at, Mr. Conway?'

He moved irritably. 'Why don't you call me Philip? Your sister does. Mr. Conway! I'm not Methuselah.'

'I didn't imply you're old, it's just I'm being respectful.' And to keep a distance between them, though that she did not say, but he understood her perfectly.

'You can't expect to keep me at arm's length, you know, not since I've played opposite to you and kissed your four nights running.'

She lowered her head and blushed fiercely.

'Then we were in a play, now everything's different.'

'Is it? Very well, I won't argue the point now.' He dropped his bantering manner and said seriously:

'I want you to play Juliet in my production at the Regina.'

'I couldn't,' she returned promptly without a second's hesitation.

'Surely that's for me to decide?'

'I think Lady Raydon must have given you an exaggerated idea of my capabilities,' she said sagely. 'Thank you for an enormous compliment, Mr. Conway, but it wouldn't do.'

'Why not? You're exactly what I want for my Juliet —gloriously young and unaffected, innocent, and yet you have incipient passion. You've had enough experience in your tinpot theatre to make you capable of sustaining a leading part.'

Though tremendously flattered that he should be prepared to engage her for such an important role, Averil was not in the least tempted to accept it. London and theatreland would be alien country to her, and the thought of being directed by Philip, however kind he promised to be, frightened her. She hated crowds and was shy of strangers. In Elmsford most of its inhabitants were known to her. She could not walk down the village street without encountering a friendly face. Philip's cast would not be friendly to a young upstart, they would resent her, that she realised at once if he did not, but he would not care while she would wilt in the chilly atmosphere, and there was John.

Seeing she was unimpressed, Philip said insinuatingly:

'The salary you'd be paid would give a tremendous boost to your savings for the mortgage and whatnot.'

That had not yet occurred to her.

'Then when the production's over I could come home and go on as before?' she asked childishly.

'If you wanted to, though I was hoping that if you're a success you'd go on. There's a modern play in which I'm interested with a part that would suit you. Once you've made a start...'

'No,' she interrupted quickly. 'I couldn't be separated from John and Elmsford indefinitely.'

Again he had to check his exasperation with her. She seemed to have no idea of the tremendous opportunity being offered to her. He knew of dozens of young actresses who would give their eye teeth for such a chance. Repressing a desire to tell her to take it or leave it, he argued, cajoled and reasoned with her, finding somewhat to his chagrin what seemed to have most weight with her was the money she could earn to bring forward her marriage.

'At least think it over,' he urged. 'I'll still be here for several days so you needn't decide now. Consult your family and John, I'm sure they'll advise you to accept.'

That Averil consented to do, but beyond that she

would make no promises, and Philip had to be content.

Averil was incapable of keeping such momentous news to herself. She blurted the whole proposition out at teatime, soon after her return, when they were all assembled round the table in the living room. Her news was received in stunned silence. Then Mr. Avon said:

'At last someone appreciates our Avvy. I'm only surprised some talent scout hasn't spotted her before, and I always felt she was wasted with the Thespians.'

'I haven't said I'll accept,' Averil reminded him.

'If you don't, you ought to have your head examined,' Cecily exclaimed. 'Surely you're not that crazy?'

'I suppose it's a great opportunity,' Mrs. Avon said doubtfully.

'Great! It's marvellous, out of this world,' Cecily cried. 'How can you hesitate for one moment?'

Averil was watching John. He was frowning, and the look he gave her was full of suspicion.

'I'd like a word with you alone after tea,' he told her.

'Of course,' she agreed.

'You can't be going to raise objections,' Cecily protested violently. 'You're utterly selfish if you do.'

John said nothing.

Alone in the Avons' small front room that was only used upon special occasions, he announced angrily:

'So this is what you and he have been hatching. I might have known you were up to something!'

'We haven't been hatching anything,' Averil declared. 'I'd no idea Mr. Conway had any such intention. I was completely taken by surprise.'

'I suppose you're raring to go?'

'No, I'm not. It's ... frightening. The only reason why I'm considering it at all is because the money I'd earn would be such a help towards our savings.'

For a moment John appeared to waver, his brown eyes had a thoughtful look, then his brow darkened and he said forcibly:

'There wouldn't be any marriage. You'd forget all about me when you got among Mr. Conway's crowd.'

'John, how can you say such a thing? I couldn't ever forget you,' she cried reproachfully. Contrarily his opposition was causing her to find Philip's offer more attractive, and she went on reasonably: 'After all, it wouldn't be for very long. As soon as the run of the play's over, and it might fold at once, I'd be back in Elmsford.'

'Would you? I doubt it. Once that skunk's got you under his thumb, he'll never let you go again.'

'Oh, that's absurd,' she exclaimed, with a faint suspicion that John might be speaking the truth. 'You've no call to abuse Mr. Conway because he admires my acting.'

'Is it only your acting?'

'But of course.' She stared at him wide-eyed. 'You can't possibly imagine I'd appeal to him as a girl? Why, he meets hundreds of lovely sophisticated women in his profession and he regards me as a naïve child who happens to possess a talent that she's too stupid to develop herself.' She blushed faintly. 'That sounds vain, but I must have something or he'd never have offered me Juliet.'

John looked at her sombrely, seeing her as a stranger might see her, and realised that the schoolgirl with whom he had been familiar for so long was developing into a very attractive woman. That creamy skin of hers, her big dark eyes that were so expressive, the sensitive mouth were all assets he had not fully valued before.

'You've got plenty,' he told her, 'and he may find

your naïveté and innocence refreshing.'

She recalled Philip's flowery remark about a crystal pool, but surely he had only meant that she was not mercenary.

'He knows Gemma Knowles,' she said almost with awe. 'You know, that lovely girl we saw in a television play. He could have had her for Juliet, but extraordinary to relate he prefers me.' She giggled. 'It's only because I look like a schoolgirl. He's got a thing about Juliet being very young.'

'Too young to be thrown among wolves,' John told her heavily, and proceeded to give her a lecture about the temptations of stage life, culled from hearsay, for he knew nothing about it first hand. Averil listened meekly in silence, thinking John would become pompous when he was elderly, and then felt contrite for the unkind thought. When he had finished she said quietly:

'Don't worry, John. If you don't want me to accept of course I won't. I'm not keen on the idea myself,' and she wondered why she was suddenly conscious of a sense of deprivation.

To Cecily's urgent insistence, she replied that she could not consider acceptance because John was dead against it.

'Damn John!' Cecily exploded. 'He's a jealous prig, making you turn down a chance in a million. Why must you consider him?'

'Because I love him and we're going to be married.'

'More's the pity,' Cecily muttered below her breath, and decided that something must be done to persuade John. She lay awake for a long time that night seeking a solution.

Averil decided she would write her refusal to Philip rather than see him again. She did not want to have to expose herself to further arguments and persuasions.

On the Monday morning she composed her letter during lulls in her work. She need not go into further explanations, she would express her gratitude and simply say it was impossible for her to accept the part. She always came home for lunch, and when she had made a pretence of eating, for all appetite had left her, she went up to her bedroom to write her note. She would post it on her way back to her office.

'Dear Mr. Conway,' she began, and smiled wryly, recalling how he had objected to that formality, but in the circumstances, it would be better not to use his first name. She was putting the few lines in her still unformed script into an envelope when Cecily came into the room. This was a surprise, for her sister worked at a distance and did not usually return at lunch time.

'Is that a definite refusal?' Cecily asked, eyeing the envelope.

'Yes.'

She sealed the flap, shutting inside it her regrets, for she did regret this final break with Philip.

'Oh well, it's your funeral,' Cecily said flippantly. 'I've been given the afternoon off.' She omitted to mention that she had asked for it on plea of important business. 'I'm going up past the Towers so I'll drop it in for you. It'll save a stamp and he'll get it more quickly.'

'Thanks.' Averil handed the missive to her; she wanted to get the matter settled as soon as possible. She went back to her office, and Cecily sauntered towards the Towers. Inside the gates she saw Philip driving his car towards her. She held up her hand and he came to stop beside her. After a short exchange, he opened the door for her and she got in beside him. The car sped away from the village at a rapid pace.

Two days later a somewhat sheepish John called in the evening, and told Averil he had changed his mind and thought she should accept Philip's offer and go to London.

'Cecily tells me she's going with you,' he said to Averil's astonishment, 'so you won't be alone, and everyone seems to think I'm standing in your way. After all, you'll be getting a big salary and it would be wonderful if we could get married sooner than we expected.'

Averil was completely taken aback by this change of front. She had been trying to settle back into her normal routine, banishing Philip sternly from her thoughts.

'It's too late,' she said dully. 'I wrote definitely refusing.'

'I don't think Mr. Conway took your refusal as final,' John informed her. 'At least Cecily says not.'

'Cis? What's she been up to, and what's this about her coming to London?'

'Oh, she's been waiting to tell you about that until I'd said my piece,' John explained hurriedly. 'It seems she's persuaded your director to give her a walk on in the play, so you'll be living together. It's a good idea.'

'But when did she see Mr. Conway?'

'I don't know, you'd better ask her.'

'It seems quite a lot's been going on behind my back,' Averil said slowly, not altogether liking this interference in her affairs. What could have her sister said to Philip, and was she in some way responsible for John's changed attitude?

'Cecily's always been dead set upon getting to London,' John observed vaguely, 'but that's enough about her. What I wanted to tell you is that I'll be seeing you every weekend when you go. I've decided I can't wait any longer to get a car and—er—' he looked faintly embarrassed, 'a friend is going to lend me enough to make up my savings to get a decent one. So I'll be able to bring you home every weekend, London's no distance really, and we shan't be parted.'

'That's fine, but, John dear, you oughtn't to run into debt.'

'Oh, it won't be a lot. I'd saved more than I thought I had, I'll soon pay it off.'

Averil looked at him doubtfully, having received a strong impression that he was concealing something that he did not want her to know, but she forgot it as she realised that her strongest bulwark against Philip's influence had collapsed. She was being pushed into a situation where she would be entirely under his domination and in daily contact with him. Up to now she had not dared to admit to herself that he held a fatal fascination for her, and the only way that she could escape involvement with him was not to see him again, but she was under no delusion that he took any personal interest in her beyond his desire to exploit her talent.

But now John beat down her further protests, being as eager to urge her to go as he had previously been determined to stop her, and with her last support gone, she could only surrender to her fate, for she could not tell him that she feared Philip's attraction, and she might well get over it upon closer acquaintance.

As soon as John had gone she went in search of her sister and found her alone in the kitchen making a cup of tea.

'You have been busy, haven't you?' she said accusingly. 'I suppose you did deliver my letter?'

'Into his own hand,' Cecily told her brightly. 'I met him in the grounds and you can't blame me for putting in a word for myself. He wasn't all that keen at first, didn't want too many Avons around, I suppose, but I was able to make a few helpful suggestions which seem to have worked, and I pointed out that if you had me with you to hold your hand, you wouldn't fret.'

'What were the helpful suggestions?' Averil demanded suspiciously, feeling that somehow she and John had been out-manoeuvred.

'Nothing he couldn't have thought of himself, given time,' Cecil said airily. She glanced mischievously at Averil's troubled face. 'Come on, Avvy, have a cuppa, and take that funereal look off your phiz.' She caught her sister round the waist and waltzed her round the room. 'Cheer up, darling, you and I are going to have fun!'

Her gaiety was infectious, and soon Averil was laughing with her over their cups of tea. Intimidating the future might be, but it was also exciting, and she would see Philip again.

CHAPTER FOUR

AVERIL was in no haste to tell Philip that she had changed her mind, or more correctly that John had changed his. In spite of what John had said, she thought he had more probably accepted her refusal and returned to town. Though the thought left her feeling a little flat, it would also be a relief. However, Cecily had no intention of letting her chance slip, and was better informed about Philip's movements than her sister was. Somehow she contrived to let him know Averil was available.

He turned up at the Avons' house one evening before she had returned from work, and she found him waiting for her in their front room. Her heart beat fast when her mother told her he was there. She went in to him clutching desperately at her composure, dressed in the simple suit she wore to work, her hair tied back and looking more like a nervous schoolgirl than an incipient actress.

Philip was standing with his back to the window, his hands thrust into his trouser pockets, apparently examining the sentimental picture of young ladies in flimsy gowns being ogled by attendant swains that hung over the sideboard.

'Here you are at last,' he said as she came timidly through the door with a murmured greeting that was quite inaudible. 'Sit down, I won't keep you long.' He glanced again at the picture with a wry smile. 'I see your family don't patronise avant-garde art.'

'That was Granny's,' Averil told him, seating herself on a hard chair. 'So it has a sentimental value for my mother.'

'I see. I understand you've revoked this.' He threw a piece of paper on to the table in front of her and she recognised her letter. 'I'm glad to learn you've come to your senses.'

His manner was abrupt and impersonal; evidently now he had obtained what he wanted he was not going to waste any of his charm upon her. His attitude dispelled her nervousness and she returned coolly:

'I wouldn't go against John's wishes, but now he's had second thoughts.'

Philip's lips curled scornfully. 'Admirable wife you'll make,' he observed drily. 'You'll be the perfect doormat.'

She disdained to respond to that remark. Sitting very straight on her chair, she enquired what he wished to see her about.

'There is a business angle to our connection,' he said

sarcastically. He sat down on the corner of the table, and produced a paper from his breast pocket. 'This is your provisional contract, the terms of which I'd better expound to you.'

He proceeded to do so, and the salary he mentioned made her gasp.

'Am I really worth all that?'

'That's nothing to what you'll be offered if you're a success, and you'll find London is an expensive place. Lady Raydon knows someone with whom you and your sister can lodge. I'll ask her to let you have the address.'

'It's still a long time off, perhaps it won't come off after all,' she suggested dubiously.

'It will. The things I undertake always do,' he assured her confidently. Then for the first time he smiled. 'Meanwhile, enjoy your summer, child, get plenty of fresh air and build up your strength for the arduous months ahead.'

She signed the form where he showed her after calling in Mrs. Avon to witness her signature.

'Doesn't Cecily get one too?' she asked as he folded the paper.

'She can wait, it's you I want to make sure of. My whole production will be inspired by you, Averil.'

She looked alarmed. 'I mayn't be adequate.'

'You will be under my direction.' Averil suppressed an inward shiver. 'You possess the first essential—youth.'

He left her with a formal handshake and a heart full of foreboding, but as spring passed into summer, her fears evaporated. *Romeo and Juliet* was scheduled to open in September and rehearsals would not start until August, which seemed to her to be aeons away, and in spite of Philip's confidence, it was possible that the production would never get off the ground. Meanwhile her life went on as before as if Philip had never come to Elmsford, except for John's car. He had bought a nearly new model Rover, which he exhibited with pride, and a Sunday drive became part of her routine. He took her to Thetford and its forest, Kersey, most enchanting of villages with its water splash across its centre and the church on the hill, and alternatively the coast. She enjoyed these expeditions, but John seemed to be subtly changing. By trade he was a joiner, which had made him such an asset to the Thespians when it came to constructing props and scenery, but now he announced that he had lost interest in the society since Averil could no longer belong to it, and as the ownership of a car had given him increased self-confidence, he managed to procure a job as a motor salesman which he considered gave him increased status. Formerly a quiet, self-effacing young man, he was becoming increasingly aggressive.

'That John of yours is getting a bit above himself,' Cecily remarked to her one day.

'You used to call him a stick-in-the-mud,' Averil reminded her, 'yet now he's launching out, you're critical. He used to be too quiet. Success has gone to his head a little.'

'A little! It's swelled up like a balloon.'

'You never have been fair to him,' Averil rebuked her. 'You should be glad he's getting on so well.'

Had she been honest she would have admitted that she had preferred John as he used to be, for he seemed to be going further away from her, though with his better prospects and her promised increased earnings, their marriage was becoming possible in the near future, and they went to look at several housing estates in the process of construction.

'When *Romeo and Juliet* is over we might be able to afford a house,' she said hopefully, looking at the patchwork of brick foundations which represented the homes-to-be. 'It just depends how long it runs.'

But she was finding the prospect of living with John in one of those little boxes no longer as alluring as it once had been.

Averil told her employers that she would be leaving after her holidays. Morton and Ramsden were a small firm of solicitors who specialised in farm business which was why their offices were in Elmsford. Mr. Morton, the senior partner, looked at her sadly.

'I suppose you're getting married,' he said. 'When we get an efficient girl that always seems to happen, but a great many women go on working afterwards nowadays.'

'I'm afraid that won't be possible,' Averil told him.

'There'll always be a place for you here if you want to come back,' he informed her.

'Thank you, Mr. Morton, that's good to know, and perhaps I will, but I haven't gone yet.'

Difficult to realise she would be far away from conveyances and law books in a few weeks' time and another girl would be sitting at her desk, using her typewriter, especially as her future seemed so fantastic. That was why she had not told Mr. Morton what she had been engaged to do, for she doubted if he would believe her, she could hardly believe it herself.

She tried to visualise life in the theatre and endeavoured to pump Lady Raydon about it, for it would be very different from their amateur productions, but Lady Raydon was not at all forthcoming, nor did she often see her alone, for she found she was no longer made welcome as she once had been. Georgina was busy organising readings to select a play for her autumn production and to find successors to Averil and Cecily. That she was excluded from these sessions gave Averil a pang, but naturally she could not expect to participate in them as she was leaving. Ever since she was sixteen she had been in Lady Raydon's productions and unreasonably she felt cast out, especially as the frequent invitations to visit the Towers had ceased. She had thought that Georgina would be delighted that Philip had engaged her to play Juliet, particularly as she had more or less engineered it by making her read some of the part, but to her disappointment, Lady Raydon seemed to resent Philip's offer. Averil's tentative suggestion that she would like to go over the part with her met with a cold refusal.

'I couldn't possibly do that. Philip will have his own ideas, and he'd be furious if I gave you a contrary interpretation.'

'Yes, I can see that. Oh, Lady Raydon, do you think I'll be all right?'

Georgina shrugged her shoulders. 'Presumably he thinks so. I'll admit I made a mistake when I encouraged you to show off, but his scornful attitude towards my theatre needled me. But I never dreamed he'd ... take you away from me.' The break in her sentence indicated that she had been going to say something else, and the grey eyes regarding the distressed girl were inimical. But Averil did not notice her expression, for her own eyes had filled with tears as she recalled her long and happy association with this woman.

'I'd much rather stay with you,' she whispered.

'Rubbish, child, take what the gods send and be thankful,' Georgina told her brusquely. 'And that reminds me, Philip asked me to give you an address for lodgings. Rachel Reubens is an old associate of mine. She possesses an old house in Bloomsbury, a legacy from her deceased husband, and she augments her income by taking in lodgers, preferably professionals.'

She wrote down the address upon a piece of mono-grammed paper. 'She's a bit of a weirdie,' she went on, 'but she'll look after you and her terms are moderate.'

Averil slipped the paper into her bag while she thanked her warmly.

'Don't thank me,' Lady Raydon said sharply. 'The least I can do is to ensure you're suitably accom-modated after getting you into this.' She gave the girl a keen penetrating look. 'He took you out to lunch, didn't he?'

'Who?' Averil asked with a fine show of indifference, though she knew very well who was meant. The village grapevine must have relayed the information to the Towers, and for some reason it had displeased the chatelaine.

'Philip, of course. If you're wise you won't let your-self become involved with him apart from the theatre. I've known Philip for a great many years, and he can be a devil.'

A look of consternation crossed her face, and she put her carefully manicured hand to her mouth as if to belatedly restrain the words that had escaped.

'I shouldn't have said that. He's no worse than other men, but be on your guard.'

'Mr. Conway knows that I'm engaged,' Averil re-turned, flushing with embarrassment. 'I shan't let him forget it, but surely he ... I ... I mean, he thinks I'm a child.'

'Yes, of course,' Georgina said hastily. 'And he re-spects innocence. Forget what I said.'

That was the last intimate conversation Averil had with Lady Raydon, and it stuck in her mind. The warning she dismissed as unnecessary, her last inter-view with Philip had been cold and businesslike, and so he would continue to be, but Lady Raydon had betrayed that she was not pleased by the turn of events, and Averil hardly flattered herself that it was the loss of her leading lady that was needling her. It sounded more like pique. She began to wonder what had transpired between Philip and her beautiful and elegant ladyship that had caused her to refer to him as a devil. But if there had been anything it was shrouded in the mists of passing years, and there could only be friendship between the respected lady of the manor and her former associate.

Averil had an uneasy suspicion that Georgina had divined her own reaction to the director and feared she might betray it to him with disastrous results, for she knew she was not as wholly indifferent to Philip as she would like to be. The three nights of the play were a golden oasis in her somewhat colourless existence. In vain she insisted to herself that it was merely the glamour of the stage that had caught her. Off-stage he was much less attractive, not so handsome, until she recalled their lunch together. No one could have been more charming than he had been then until he had approached his real object in inviting her, and then the ruthless streak had shown, as it had done when he inveigled her into his car. Again and again Lady Raydon's words returned to her. 'He can be a devil.'

Studying the text of one of the most famous love stories in the world she found echoes in the passionate words, though she could never achieve the Italian girl's reckless disregard of consequences. But Romeo was nearly as young and quite as violently passionate as his inamorata. Philip was a mature man with a cynical view of women and love. There was no comparison there, and as she had told Lady Raydon, he regarded Averil as a child, and a naïve and tiresome one at that, who could only redeem herself in his sight by intense application to her work. Her obsession would fade in time and daily contact with him would be disillusioning, or so she hoped, and she must never let John gain an inkling that her fancy had strayed. Dear faithful John, who was working so hard to make a home for them, she could not let him down, and mercifully he had not appeared to notice her slight shrinking from his kisses, or if he had he would attribute it to maidenly reserve. He was nearly as immature as herself regarding sex, she thought almost angrily; he had no knowledge of the strange hungry emotions coming to birth in her, feelings that would shock him horribly and shocked herself.

Now that he had more money, John suddenly woke up to the fact that he had never given her a ring, excusing this omission by declaring that he had wanted to wait until he could give her a good one. There had been no hurry with their marriage so far distant, and both sets of parents declaring that they were too young, but now Averil was going to live among strangers, he was anxious that she should wear his token. They went to a shop in Bury and she chose a half-hoop of brilliants, but the price caused her to gasp. John insisted she must have it, and he could afford it.

'I want you to have a ring that looks something when you get among your fine stage colleagues,' he told her as they left the shop, 'and I'm getting a good screw now.'

'It's lovely, John.' She spread her fingers the better to admire it. 'But I don't think we should squander money too recklessly, we've the future to save for.' He must still owe a considerable amount on the car.

John laughed. 'My pet, you don't know how to squander anything, and the future can take care of itself.'

Apprehension struck her at this very uncharacteristic remark. As she got into the car, she asked:

'But you do still want to marry me, John? You

aren't having second thoughts?'

'Dear goose, of course not. Haven't I just given you my pledge? It's you who may be having them in this exciting new life of yours.'

'It won't make any difference,' she said feverishly, as he fixed his seat belt. 'I won't let it make any difference. Oh, darling John you're my mainstay, my anchor.' And she flung her arms about him.

'Mind the steering wheel,' he cautioned her, overwhelmed by the fervour of her embrace. He kissed her awkwardly and disentangled himself, a dark flush of embarrassment staining his face. 'It's rather public here, my pet.'

Chilled, she drew back, mechanically fastening her belt. She saw he was looking about anxiously, wondering if any passer by had noticed her behaviour, as if embracing in a car were a heinous offence, and surely it must be common enough. She was aware of intense irritation. Her impulsive action had been an appeal for help against her infatuation for Philip, and she turned the new ring upon her finger, thinking John should have followed its bestowal with a little more ardour. She glanced at him and saw he was looking at his face in the driving mirror to see if she had left any lipstick smudge upon it. Actually she had not been wearing any. As he started the car she began to wonder if he were capable of any real ardour. Certainly he bore little resemblance to Romeo.

The summer passed with increasing acceleration and finally August was there, and the girls were due in London. John drove them up in his car on the Sunday night before they were called to rehearsal. Cecily was excited and chattered all the way, but Averil sat silent beside John with a sense of doom, which increased with every mile. Cecily's small part carried no responsibility, but Averil's was immense. If she failed she supposed Gemma Knowles could replace her, but she had no wish to fail.

Mrs. Reubens turned out to be fat and good-natured with a Jewish cast of countenance. In her youth she had been handsome, but her early good looks had soon deteriorated. She showed the girls with some pride the large, high-ceilinged room on the second floor which was to be theirs. The windows looked out on to the square round which the houses were built, with a rather dreary garden in its centre full of sad-looking dusty trees.

'Nice to be able to look at a bit of green,' she said, indicating them. 'I hope you'll be happy with me, dearies. At least I'm used to theatrical hours and know what meals you'll be needing, but I won't stand for any wild parties in my house, nor men stopping all night.'

'I can promise you there won't be anything like that,' Averil exclaimed quickly. 'We aren't those sort of girls.'

'I didn't mean to give offence,' their hostess apologised. 'You're from the country, aren't you? You don't know what young folk get up to these days, and it's as well to have a clear understanding right from the start.'

John brought up their cases and Mrs. Reubens invited him to share their evening meal.

'Which is only cold meat, as it's Sunday,' she warned him.

John declined, saying he must get back. Since there would be no performances during the weeks of rehearsal he would come to fetch them next Saturday afternoon. He was awkward and bashful, overawed by Mrs. Reubens, whose bulk intimidated him, nor did he wholly approve of her; she appeared to him to be blowsy.

'Write as soon as you can, darling,' he mumbled into Averil's neck as he kissed her cheek chastely under Mrs. Reubens' curious gaze. 'I'll be thinking of you.'

Averil watched him drive away with a sinking heart. The last dear and familiar thing had gone.

'Your brother?' Mrs. Reubens enquired.

'Oh no, my fiancé.'

'Really?' The good lady looked surprised.

'John isn't one to wear his heart upon his sleeve,' Cecily informed her with a mischievous gleam in her eyes.

Mrs. Reubens nodded. 'The cold reserved Englishman,' she observed. 'So dampening. I like a bit of emotion myself. How can a woman be sure she's loved when her fellow behaves like a codfish?'

'John isn't very demonstrative,' Averil said defensively.

Mrs. Reubens chuckled. 'Bit shy, eh? Personally I'm all for the bold ones, they're much more fun. My poor Samuel was as bold as brass.'

They were given the threatened cold meat and salad for supper in the communal dining room, where only two other people were present.

'Most of 'em go out at weekends,' Mrs. Reubens explained. 'Those two ladies are here only temporarily while they're resting between shows.'

The two ladies were a couple of faded specimens of womanhood who looked as if they would be resting for some time. The glances they threw at the two young girls were not very friendly.

'Soured and embittered,' Cecily whispered to her sister, but Averil said: 'Poor things,' with genuine compassion.

After their meal they had the choice of going to the sitting room, which boasted a television or to their own room. Cecily halfheartedly suggested going out, but with the ordeal of the next morning pressing upon her spirits, Averil had no wish to do so. She said she was tired and would unpack. Even the effervescent Cecily was feeling a little subdued amidst their strange surroundings. Averil said suddenly as they went upstairs:

'Thank heaven you've been engaged too, Cis. I don't know how I could have borne it alone.'

Cecily laughed. "If it hadn't been for me you wouldn't have been here at all,' she said incautiously.

Averil looked at her wonderingly, but at that moment Mrs. Reubens' stentorian voice wafted up the stairs towards them vibrant with excitement.

'Girls! Girls! There's a gentleman to see you.'

They looked at each other.

'Whoever——?' Cecily asked.

But suddenly Averil knew. She turned about and ran down the stairs towards the figure standing below her. He, disdaining to wait in the sitting room, was watching her descent. She caught her foot in the carpet nearly at the bottom and tumbled straight into his arms.

Philip had no inhibitions about possible onlookers, or probably kissing was so commonplace with him that he thought nothing of it. Nor was he content with chaste salutes upon the cheek. Averil found herself held close against him and the pressure of his lips hard upon her own. For a second, her apprehensions, John, everything was blotted from her mind in a moment of pure rapture, the cause of which she had no chance to analyse, for Philip pushed her gently away from him and said casually:

'Welcome to the big city, and I hope you're prepared to work hard and long.' Words that did not match his actions.

Mrs. Reubens said from somewhere behind them

with ghoulish satisfaction:

'The Maestro has the reputation of being a slave-driver and reducing all his actresses to tears.'

'Shall I make you cry?' Philip asked Averil, tracing the line of her cheek with his forefinger.

'I hope not, and I don't cry easily,' Averil told him nervously.

Cecily joined them, but rather to her sister's surprise she made no attempt to claim a salute from Philip, saying flippantly:

'All hail, lord and master. Have you come to make sure the goods have been delivered safely and in good condition?'

'You, my girl, will have to learn to control that pert tongue of yours,' he returned, but with perfect good humour. He swung round on his heel. 'Come on, Rachel, you old elephant, what about some coffee, or have you something stronger to celebrate my leading lady's arrival?'

Mrs. Reubens grinned. 'So it's like that, is it?'

'What do you mean, "like that", you old besom? I'd have you know Averil is a little innocent flower with no knowledge of the wicked ways of our swinging city. Don't you dare to try to corrupt her.'

'Oh, Maestro, as if I would!'

Obviously they were well known to each other and the old woman enjoyed his chaffing.

'I wouldn't put it past you,' he remarked. 'What about that drink?'

'I know what you like, but the young ladies had better have coffee.'

'If you're going to produce my favourite tipple, I agree.'

'Then go into my private room,' she commanded. 'There we won't be interrupted.'

She removed her large bulk, in spite of which she

could move with noiseless speed and Philip ushered his protégées into her sanctum, with which he seemed to be familiar. This was a small, over-furnished room with worn but comfortable sofa and chairs. The walls and every available space were covered with signed photographs which represented several decades in theatrical history. Pride of place was given to a large silver-framed picture of the 'bold' Samuel on a Victorian escritoire.

'A bit of a mausoleum,' Philip remarked, glancing round, 'most of the people represented are dead. But Rachel will make you comfortable, and she's most respectable.'

'To guard your innocent flowers?' Cecily asked cheekily. 'I'm not sure I care for that description. We do know the facts of life.'

She seated herself in an armchair, while Averil placed herself on the sofa, which being back against the wall was as far from Philip as she could get. He stood on the hearthrug and continued to spar good-temperedly with Cecily. Averil sat silent, watching Philip's face with yearning intensity. She had not seen him for several months and she was seeking to re-familiarise herself with his features. He looked a little thinner and was very bronzed, the fair hair being several tones lighter than his skin. He must have been abroad or at sea. In contrast to the brown hue of his face his eyes were startlingly blue. He wore a formal dark suit with a white shirt, gold cuff links and watch strap, which would indicate he had been to some function. He looked very much the well dressed man about town with no suggestion of the Bohemian world of the theatre. For the first time she wondered vaguely about his means. Drama directors, even famous ones, were not excessively well paid. Yet Philip always appeared affluent. The suit he was wearing had been shaped by a master tailor, and the car he had driven had been an expensive model. She rather suspected that he had contributed generously towards the financing of the production of *Romeo and Juliet*.

Mrs. Reubens returned with the coffee and a bottle of brandy.

'You see, I never forget your favourite brand, Maestro.'

'Do you keep it in store for my infrequent visits?'

'Not so infrequent. You always remember your old friends.'

'I can't afford to forget friends as staunch as you, Rachel.'

She sighed and subsided into the armchair opposite to Cecily. 'Ah well, we've had our good times as well as some bad. Why don't you sit down, Mr. Philip?'

'Thanks, but I've been driving most of the day and I'm glad to stand.'

'Then would one of you young ladies pour the coffee? My feet ache.'

Cecily immediately started to pour out.

'Averil seems lost in a dream,' she observed. 'My sister is a great dreamer, Mrs. Reubens.'

Rachel looked curiously at the quiet girl sitting aloof. She had marked the change in her when Philip had appeared. Eyes and lips had flown signals which any experienced woman could read. Yet she had introduced the very ordinary young man who had brought her as her fiancé.

'What does she play in your production, Maestro?' she asked, when Cecily had handed her her coffee and taken a cup across to Averil.

Philip, in the act of pouring out his drink, said casually:

'Juliet.'

'So you were not joking when you said she was your

leading lady? But she has no well known name to put up in the lights.'

He returned tersely: 'She's young.'

'Ah, you always did have that obsession with a young Juliet, but Juliet must have fire and passion.'

He said, with his eyes upon the contents of his glass.

'Averil is a dark horse, but I'm certain she will surprise us all, including herself.'

'You should know, Maestro,' Mr. Reubens said doubtfully.

'Of course I know.'

He looked at Averil, who was miserably examining her nails, the untouched coffee on the occasional table beside her. He was so confident about her success, but she did not believe she had the fire and passion Rachel had mentioned that were so necessary for the part. Philip had only seen her play Phoebe Throssel, and that was something quite different, a light comedy part, which though it was supposed to be the most difficult form of acting to put over did not require the emotional intensity of Juliet.

'Don't let my dolorous elephant discourage you,' Philip said kindly. 'I'm certain I can get what I want from you.'

'Yes,' Rachel affirmed, nodding her head. 'Your tactics are well known. She won't be able to call her soul her own. The good Lord help the poor girl!'

A second's pause followed this pronouncement while they all looked uneasily at the fat old woman, who had the air of a prophetess. Then Philip laughed a little forcedly and walking across to Averil, sat down on the sofa beside her.

'I'm not a monster, Averil,' he told her lightly. 'Though Rachel is implying that I am. I promise again I'll deal gently with you.'

She raised scared eyes to his face. 'Please do,' she

whispered.

He patted her hand in a paternal manner. 'Only trust me.'

But his blue eyes were hard and cold.

She said simply: 'I will because I must. I'm in your hands.' And she remembered Lady Raydon had called him a devil.

'What's got into you all?' Cecily cried gaily, breaking the tension which seemed to have arisen. 'You look like the tragic muse, Avvy, and you ought to be full of the joys of spring. Here's to your success!' She waved her coffee cup. 'Why didn't Shakespeare put more women into his plays, Philip, then I might have had a decent part instead of being a page or some such.'

'Because in his time there were no women on the stage, as you should know,' Philip told her. 'The female parts were played by boys; nowadays girls often walk on as boys.'

'Shall I wear tights?' She pulled up her short skirt even higher to regard her shapely legs. 'I was hoping to give the boys a thrill.'

'You're an optimist! We see far too many female legs nowadays to be thrilled, and most of them would be better covered up. But my production is going to be ultra-modern, as I believe I've mentioned, so you may end up in jeans.'

'How dull!' Cecily made a grimace. 'Isn't there anything female in the play besides Ladies Capulet and Montague and the nurse?'

Philip grinned mischievously. 'There's Rosaline.'

Cecily, who had not read the full text, demanded to know who she might be.

'Romeo's first love, but she doesn't appear unless I put her into the party scene, but if I do it'll only be a walk-on.'

'So you were teasing,' Cecily laughed. 'But did

Romeo have a former love? I thought his and Juliet's affair was a one-and-only business.'

'Far from it as far as he was concerned. He was infatuated with Rosaline, according to his friends, and made the switch to Juliet very quickly, which didn't augur well for their future together had they lived.'

A typical Philip Conway remark, Averil thought; how many times had he fallen in and out of love? She glanced at him curiously, wondering if there were a present object of his affections, though affection was hardly the right word to use for what Philip would feel for a woman. However many he had known, he had managed to avoid matrimony as far as she knew. Possibly, in spite of his cynicism, he was still faithful to that first love the existence of which she had divined, an idea which she found more acceptable than that he was merely promiscuous.

As if sensing her interest, Philip lay back on the sofa and laid his hand over hers lying in her lap, a warm reassuring clasp, while he continued to exchange further banter with Cecily. Averil remained silent, aware only of the lean brown fingers holding hers. Tired with the long day and her new impressions, she was conscious only of their contact, being lulled into a sort of dreamy content. Some mesmeric influence seemed to flow from him into her with the touch of his hand, allaying her fears. That he was aware of it and had deliberately engendered it did not occur to her.

Then with a swift change of mood, Philip broke off his light repartee and said severely:

'Nevertheless, Cecily, you will remember that in the theatre I'm boss, and though I've indulged you tonight, I shall expect respect and obedience from you there.'

'Of course,' Cecily agreed. 'You needn't be so ogreish about it.'

'So long as you understand. I'd hate to have to reprimand you in public.'

He released Averil's hand, and rose to his feet. He had transformed himself from the friendly welcomer to the aloof dictator in the matter of minutes.

'I must be off now,' he told them. 'I'll see you in the morning, young ladies—and please not to be late.' He went to Rachel and his face softened as he dropped a kiss upon her greying hair. 'Look after my chickens, elephant, and if there's any insubordination, let me know at once.' The blue gaze flickered over them with an admonitory glance. 'Take care of yourself, Rachel.'

He was gone without a formal leavetaking.

'Insubordination ... chickens!' Cecily exploded. 'What the hell does he think we are?'

'A pair of ignorant girls,' Mrs. Reubens said placidly. 'You've got a lot to learn, my dears. Might I suggest an early night? Tomorrow will be an exacting day for you both.'

When they were in bed, twin divans placed side by side, Cecily said suddenly: 'He's sweet on you, of course.'

'Who?' Averil quavered.

Cecily switched off her bedside lamp and snuggled down under her blankets.

'The lord high executioner, Mr. Philip Conway,' she said sleepily. 'You'll need to watch your step, Av.'

'He isn't,' Averil declared vehemently. 'He couldn't be,' adding with sudden insight: 'He was trying to soften me up to make me more malleable.'

But Cecily was asleep.

CHAPTER FIVE

AVERIL woke early on the fateful morning when she was to be introduced to the company at the Regina Theatre. Recalling Philip's visit on the previous evening. she looked at her still sleeping sister with faint amusement. Cecily, for all her assumption of sophistication, could be as romantic as any other teenage girl. Because Philip had sat beside her and held her hand she had attributed sentimental motives for his actions, but had she known him better she would have known that sentiment had no place in his make-up. Philip was inured to tender feelings and used people for his own ends. Being sensitive enough to understand her trepidation, he had employed his own special therapy to dispel it, but whether she could rely upon his promise to deal gently with her only time would prove. She had a nasty feeling that if she proved to be stupid and slow to grasp what he required of her he would forget to be patient.

Mrs. Reubens had warned them that informal clothes were worn at rehearsals, and any dressing up would be considered ostentatious. Averil hastened to the bathroom which she surmised, correctly as it proved, would be unoccupied at that early hour, and sought to recover her drooping spirits in a scented bath, using the fragrant bath cubes she had brought with her. She returned to the bedroom and sat in the window brushing her hair while she watched the square come to life. Blinds went up in the houses opposite, early workers ascended from basements or descended from flats; milkmen deposited their offerings upon doorsteps and postmen pushed letters through letter boxes.

Cecily yawned, stretched and sat up.

'Up already!' she exclaimed. 'Couldn't you sleep?'

'Oh yes, but I woke early. Cis, I feel awful.'

'Come off it, girl, they're only people, they can't eat you. A week today you'll be wondering what on earth you were so scared about.'

'I'm sure I hope so. Thank goodness you'll be there to support me.'

Although she had not been called, Cecily had been cast for Paris's page, who only speaks in the last act and in the dark, and a walk-on in the party scene; she was determined to accompany her sister, for she doubted if Averil would have the courage to make it without her. They had been notified of date and time before leaving Elmsford. Averil could only make a pretence of eating breakfast, and they set off for the theatre with a flood of good wishes from their hostess. As the weather was hot, they were wearing thin trousers and cotton tops, and carried cardigans. A short journey by tube took them to the Regina in the heart of theatreland, and they approached the stage door with butterflies in their tummies, even Cecily becoming excited. The doorkeeper directed them to a flight of stone steps, which led up to the rehearsal room, for the stage was occupied by the current production. It was a large dingy apartment at the top of the theatre which did not look as if the cleaners often visited it. Since they were a little early, they had it to themselves, and a large mirror covering one wall reflected their youthful and rather forlorn figures.

The rest of the company began to filter in, hailing each other excitedly and chattering loudly. Cecily and

Averil retreated to one of the windows overlooking the street.

'What a mob!' Cecily murmured under her breath. 'And I wonder when this place was last dusted.'

A sudden silence fell on the assembled artistes as Philip and his stage manager came into the room. He took his place behind a wooden table in front of one wall, and the stage manager spread the prompt copy of the play and his notes in front of him, as he sat beside him. Every move that Philip had plotted would have to be noted in the script, and all the 'business' he had devised. The company sat themselves down on the benches which ran round two sides of the oblong room, Averil and Cecily subsiding where they were, only to find they were directly opposite to the director's table. Philip gave them a glance as if to assure himself that they were present, but he gave no sign of recognition. He wore dark grey trousers and a grey sleeveless pullover over a blue shirt, and was freshly shaved, which many of his company were not. In spite of his casual garb he contrived to look distinguished and very much the man in command. McAllister, the stage manager, was a redhaired Celt with a profusion of whiskers and light blue eyes that had none of the metallic gleam that characterised Philip's narrower and much darker orbs. McAllister read out the list of the company's names to which they answered rather like assembly at a school. When in a barely audible voice Averil made known her presence, there was a ripple of interest through her colleagues and many curious eyes were turned in her direction. When it had been discovered that a totally unknown young woman was to play Juliet, they had drawn their own conclusions. Either she was the daughter of a rich sponsor who had made her engagement the price of his contribution, or else she was a recipient of Philip's favours, but her appearance ruled out the second supposition. That slight unsophisticated-looking creature with her fall of straight brown hair could never be fancied by a connoisseur of women as Philip Conway was known to be. She must have been foisted upon him in exchange for much-needed funds, and they looked forward to hearing him rend her into shreds. When he had fully satisfied everybody, including her misguided parent that she was hopeless, then the understudy would take over. It had happened before when Philip was directing, and Gemma Knowles who had been engaged to understudy the lead perked up. She had been disappointed she had not been offered the chief part, since she knew she had been considered for it, but now she became convinced that she would play it in the end.

Averil had darted a shy glance towards her when she had answered to her name. Gemma was a very pretty woman, with a flower-like face and golden hair that was probably dyed, but she could give Averil ten years, being near her thirtieth birthday, and her dark eyes held a disillusioned look which proclaimed that she was far from innocent. Their eyes met, and Gemma's handsome mouth curled disdainfully. On the verge of a friendly smile, Averil looked hastily away.

Philip addressed them in a few clipped sentences, outlining his plan for the production and what he would expect of them, and then proceeded to plot the moves. This was the pattern for the rest of the week. Nobody attempted to act, they merely marked the positions in their books as each scene was set. Averil was familiar with the stage vernacular, and was not disconcerted when told to move O.P. or 'break down left.' But she had always disliked rehearsing in a room, which the Thespians rarely did, having the use of their own stage, and found the bare boards with their chalk marks representing a balcony or Friar Lawrence's cell uninspiring, and the ring of onlookers excessively trying. She seemed to be right on top of them and their expressions were anything but encouraging.

Philip was completely impersonal. He addressed her as Miss Avon, a formality he only relaxed towards some of the men who were best known to him. This aloofness chilled Averil, though she did not know what else she had expected. She had understood that theatrical manners were familiar, but Philip built a fence about himself that made him inaccessible. Neither did he use the 'dears' and 'darlings' with which the rest of the company were so lavish.

Cecily explained his attitude to her own satisfaction several days later.

'He's evidently taken to heart the saying that familiarity breeds contempt,' she observed. 'He's the big noise and he doesn't mean to let us forget it, and his method works. Have you noticed that whenever he appears there's instant silence?'

'They're all afraid of his caustic comments,' Averil said. 'It doesn't make for a friendly atmosphere.'

'You needn't complain, you're the only one who seems immune from them,' Cecily told her feelingly, for she had earned for herself a sharp reprimand for giggling out of turn.

'So far,' Averil conceded, wondering how long Philip's patience with her would last, for she was painfully aware of her inexperience and self-consciousness.

Since the weather continued to be hot and sunny, both girls found the long hours confined in the dusty rehearsal room excessively trying. Averil was looking forward with passionate eagerness to the weekend when John would come to fetch them on the Saturday afternoon and she would have a night and a day in the pastoral surroundings of Elmsford. They had arranged to travel by underground to the outskirts of London so that John would not have to cope with the congested city streets. As it was he was held up by the weekend traffic and arrived late and irritable. He proposed that they should in future take the train as far as Colchester, where he could meet them with less difficulty. Averil agreed it would be a better arrangement, while she stifled her disappointment caused by John's perfunctory greeting. He seemed much more concerned with the traffic problem than pleased to see her. Also he was eyeing her trousers and tank top with faint disparagement.

Seated beside him in the car, she watched with mounting pleasure the built-up areas slide by. Soon she would be among the green fields and woods for which her senses were hungering.

John said during a hold-up at a roundabout:

'You haven't changed much, Avvy.'

'But good heavens, John, we've only been away a week! How could I have changed?'

He glanced at the pure oval of her face, the fall of soft brown hair on either side of it, noting her complete lack of make-up. He frowned with evident displeasure.

'I should have thought that now you're a pro you'd have dolled yourself up a bit,' he complained.

'We don't dress up to go to the theatre,' she told him, 'and one of the joys of coming home is that one needn't bother about one's appearance.'

'But I like to see you looking smart,' he protested. 'I've told my pals I'm engaged to an actress and they expect to see something.'

'Oh, John!' She stared at him in wide-eyed consternation. 'Don't you like me as I am, as I've always been?'

The traffic began to move, and he changed gear.

'Times change,' he said gruffly. 'You aren't a teenager any longer.'

'Very well, next time you come for us I'll give you the works,' she returned, concealing her dismay at his criticism. 'Would you perhaps fancy false eyelashes?'

He gave her a quick glance. 'You don't need 'em, your own are beautiful,' he allowed. 'Sorry, Avvy, I didn't mean to be unkind, but you don't make the best of yourself, do you?'

'That's what I'm always telling her,' Cecily chipped in from the back seat.

'You do,' John remarked.

'A girl should if she wants to get a man,' Cecily declared. 'And though you may have got yours, Avvy, you do have to work to keep 'em, you know.'

'I'm learning,' Averil said despondently, wondering if Philip would like to see her painted and polished. Somehow she felt he preferred her as she was. It was a blow that John wanted her to dress up. She came home to relax in her old things, and though she was expert with stage make-up she was not very clever with daylight applications.

John delivered them on their doorstep and suggested going out that night, but Averil said she was too tired.

'I've had a wearing week,' she excused herself.

'I suppose so,' he admitted grudgingly, and Averil thought he might have shown more understanding. 'I'll be round tomorrow afternoon and stop for tea if I may.'

'You're expected.'

'I'll stay until I have to take you to the station in the evening,' he went on, 'but I won't come in now since you're so tired.'

'John's going to find taxiing us a chore,' Cecily observed as he drove away. 'Wasn't that his excuse for buying a car?'

'Not really, it was only a side issue, so to speak.'

'And you still don't know who he borrowed from?'

'That's John's business,' Averil reproved her, as their mother came running downstairs to embrace them.

Averil went to bed early and rose late to spend most of the rest of the day sitting in a deck chair in the Avons' small square of back garden dozing. The weather was still hot and sunny, and she roused herself with difficulty when John came to join her.

'I hope life in London isn't going to be too much for you,' Mrs. Avon said anxiously, viewing her daughter's recumbent figure.

'I'll get used to it,' Averil assured her, 'it's just it's such a change at first and the heat's been so trying.'

Cecily was less affected; she sat on the grass beside John and was eager to chatter. To her mother's enquiry as to whether they had made any friends, she replied with a laugh:

'Our landlady's a lamb and a mountain of good nature, but the company hates us like poison, they consider we're interlopers.'

'Perhaps they're jealous of Mr. Conway's favour,' John insinuated, with his eyes on Averil's face.

'He doesn't show us any,' Cecily declared. 'He's the great god on Olympus and he doesn't condescend to know us off-stage.'

Averil smiled faintly, recalling how Philip had greeted them upon their arrival, but there was no need to mention that, especially as there did not seem to be much likelihood of a repetition. John was registering satisfaction as it appeared the occasional doubts he had had about Philip's intentions towards his fiancée were groundless.

As previously suggested, John took the girls only as far as Colchester to catch the last train up to town.

The train was late and while they waited on the platform a local one which usually came in after the London train had left entered the station on the further side. There were not many people travelling, so that as the passengers came over the bridge, the little group of two girls and John were easily identified. A bold-looking girl with a bush of synthetic red hair came running down the stairs and along the platform towards them. She wore a green trouser suit and her prominent eyes were heavily shaded with green make-up.

'Hi, Johnnie!' she called. 'So you've got here first.'

John looked embarrassed, and realising he was escorting the girls, the newcomer went on hastily:

'It's so difficult getting transport at this time of night, and recognising John I hoped he'd give me a lift. You're Averil Avon, aren't you? I'm Clarice Jackson, and I've often seen you act at the village theatre.'

The London train slid in before Averil could make any rejoinder, and John hurriedly bustled them into a compartment. He kissed Averil absently, then stepped back to make the usual banal remarks to her as she stood at the open window. It had been so nice seeing her again and he would meet them here next Saturday, when he hoped she would be feeling less tired. He was careful to ignore Clarice, who stood behind him, obviously waiting for him. Averil wondered if she knew that John was engaged to her.

When the train had started, Cecily remarked:

'What do you make of that?'

'Make of what?'

'That red-haired piece.'

'I don't make anything. I don't expect John to exist in a male purdah while I'm away, and why shouldn't he give her a lift?'

'No reason at all. But it was prearranged, and if the

train hadn't been late we shouldn't have seen her. He's never mentioned Clarice to us.'

'Why should he? I've complete trust in John, Cis.'

Cecily shrugged her shoulders and said no more, but she thought her sister was being wilfully blind to obvious danger signals, and Averil had already dismissed Clarice from her mind. She was making the difficult transition from one life to the other. She was leaving Elmsford with intense reluctance, for it was to her a haven of peace and security. The prospect of the Monday morning rehearsal among people who did not trouble to conceal their antagonism was not alluring. As for Philip, the remote figure in blue and grey behind the wooden table giving out sharp incised directions was a different person from the man she had formerly known almost intimately. He never as much as gave her a smile, let alone any encouragement. Having got her where he wanted her he saw no need to exert himself further to charm her. She had become another puppet under his direction, who was not supposed to have any feelings except for her role in the play.

Cecily was in a happier mood. The company were more inclined to accept her since she was so unimportant, and she had detected that the stage manager had a roving eye, which she meant to catch. Moreover, she had no love for Elmsford. Thus as they approached the city lights, her spirits rose as Averil's sank.

The next week, as they were supposed to know their positions and their words, the play began to take shape, a shape devised by its director. Philip was on the whole patient, but now and then he would utter cutting sarcastic criticisms which made the recipient wilt. Averil dreaded being their object, but so far he had remembered his promise to treat her gently and she escaped the lash of his tongue. She suffered at first from an almost paralysing self-consciousness, and the keen blue eyes looked volumes though he said nothing. She spoke her words beautifully, but she was not acting. There was no connection between what she was saying and the feeling that must come from the heart to make a part live. Her Romeo gave her little help. Nigel Forbes was a handsome young man with fine dark eyes, black hair and a reckless debonair manner, which was effective in his scenes with Mercutio and the other young men, but with her he was not good. They seemed unable to strike fire from each other. Averil was aware that he scorned her and wanted Gemma, with whom he seemed en rapport, to play the part, and fancied his stiffness with herself was deliberate.

Then one morning, Philip came out from behind his table and pushing Nigel aside took his place. It was the famous balcony scene and he knew the words without reference to the script, and as soon as he began to speak, Averil immediately responded. The dingy room and censorious eyes faded from her vision, he and she were alone together in Capulet's moonlit garden. She broke through the barrier of self-consciousness which had so hampered her, a warm flood of feeling suffused her being.

Juliet, ardent, rapturous, longing to pour out her love, yet has some qualms that she is being too forward, also that the passion which has descended upon them both 'like lightning' may not be durable. In spite of Romeo's protestations, she says when she bids him goodnight:

'This bud of love by summer's ripening breath
May prove a beauteous flower when next we meet.'

This bud of love? As Philip continued in Nigel's place, the words Averil was speaking seemed to be the voice of her own heart. Until that moment she had tried to deceive herself, but now she knew that the bud of her love was opening, but not for the absent John, it was being unfurled by the man who was simulating passion so beautifully in response to her acting. Acting! She must never betray that her emotion was not wholly assumed, for Philip would only treat her infatuation with contempt, or worse still be amused by it.

Philip played the scene through to Juliet's final exit. Then he returned to his seat and looked at Nigel.

'You see, she can do it when she has the right support, so pull your socks up, my lad.'

Nigel scowled and said something to Gemma which made her smile.

'May we hear the joke?' Philip asked suavely.

'Wasn't anything,' Nigel mumbled.

'A simple comment on the weather, perhaps?' Philip suggested with eyes like ice. 'Suppose we continue. We won't do that scene again now, but I expect it to be played properly tomorrow.'

'It will be if Miss Avon can bring herself to accept me as your substitute,' Nigel said nastily.

Someone tittered and then quailed as Philip's steely glance impaled them.

'Miss Avon will play it exactly as she has done just now,' he predicted coldly.

And Averil did. Now she had at last broken through the shell of self-consciousness that enclosed her, it did not reform, and Nigel was too good an actor not to play up to her. The scene throbbed with emotion beautifully restrained, but Philip did not praise them. That was not his way. They had obeyed his direction and he let the scene go without comnent.

A new and tormenting thought occurred to Averil. Was Philip aware of her feelings for him, had he deliberately sought to arouse it to enhance her performance? He rarely gave an actual demonstration of how a part should be played, and his action of the previous day had been prompted because he was sure he could make her respond to him exactly as she had done. She was thankful that she had been able to repeat her performance with Nigel, thus escaping the malicious glances and whispered comments of her colleagues, but she would have little chance of suppressing her growing love for Philip if he were going to continually evoke it to win from her the emotional intensity the play demanded. Lady Raydon had said he was a devil, and Averil began to perceive in what manner he could be cruel. To obtain what he wanted in his productions he would not scruple to use any means that were offered without the slightest regard for his victim's feelings, nor could she escape from him; he had her trapped.

'You were fine,' Cecily murmured as the break was called for lunch. 'He might have said so.'

'I suppose I only did what he expected,' Averil returned.

'Wouldn't have hurt him to give you a word of praise,' Cecily declared with some heat.

'He never gives that to anyone,' Averil pointed out, as Rosamund Brent, an old actress who was playing the Nurse and therefore was not in competition with the younger girls, came up to them.

'I'll admit I was astonished when I found Gemma wasn't to play Juliet,' she said, 'but I know now why Philip wanted you.' She patted Averil's arm. 'You've got the real stuff, my dear, and youth as well—radiant youth. I've seen many Juliets, but I've never seen that scene better acted.'

'Thank you,' Averil spoke with genuine gratitude. This was the first time a member of the company had shown her any friendliness.

Cecily was more fortunate, for no one envied her her few lines and she was so bright and pretty that the men in the company were already paying her attentions. She was not called for every rehearsal, not being needed, but Averil was happier when she was there, so she always came. Philip might have been led to vetoing her appearance, for she relieved her boredom by whispered comments to whoever was sitting next to her, but at last the theatre was available during the daytime and the company moved into the auditorium, where, sitting well back, she could talk as much as she chose provided she kept her voice low.

Averil was delighted to be on the stage even though it looked big and bare lighted by a few naked bulbs, and her work improved enormously, up to the point where Juliet is married to Romeo.

The scene where the banished husband at risk of his life if he is discovered climbs into his wife's bedroom is in the original text set on Juliet's balcony, but with the facilities of modern staging, directors find it more poignant if it takes place in Juliet's room, and part of the action played on the bed itself.

Try as she would, Averil could not get the right degree of emotional intensity that Philip demanded, the agony of a young bride whose lover by cruel circumstances is driven from her arms.

'You're too damned inhibited,' he told her, mercifully when no one was within earshot. 'Juliet from this point onwards is a wife. I want more abandon.'

'I . . . I'm doing my best,' Averil faltered.

'Then your best just isn't good enough. Perhaps some private coaching might help you. I'll arrange a session.'

Averil's heart leaped and sank. If she were alone with Philip could she manage not to betray herself?

The scene in question was too charged with emotion, too tense.

'It's very good of you to take so much trouble,' she said doubtfully. 'But is it really necessary?'

'I wouldn't suggest it if it wasn't.' He was irritable and on edge. 'I can't afford to let you flop. Only a success on your part will vindicate me, for I insisted upon your engagement.'

'What a pity you did,' she sighed.

'Damn it all, girl!' he exploded. 'Do you want to rake all that up again? You are engaged, and you've got to succeed, if I have to half kill you in the process!' At her scared look, he calmed himself. 'I'm convinced you can do it, child,' he went on more gently, 'with my help. The difficulty is where we can work. Obviously I can't come to your place and the theatre's occupied. Would you object to coming round to my flat?'

'Why should I?' she asked innocently. 'When should I come?'

'The sooner we get down to it the better. What about tonight at eight o'clock?'

With some trepidation she agreed.

'Good. I'm afraid I can't offer to give you a meal beforehand. I've got some business to attend to first.'

'Of course I didn't expect that,' she exclaimed.

'Didn't you?' He looked at her curiously. 'You never do expect much, do you, Averil? You shouldn't be so humble.'

She laughed. 'But I am humble, a country mouse that you're hoping to make into a star. But I'm afraid I'll only be a comet—a swift passage and then oblivion.'

'We'll see about that when the time comes,' he returned. 'Perhaps I won't let you pass into oblivion. Meanwhile we've got to make certain you do become a star. Eight o'clock, then, and here's the address.' He handed her his card. 'Oh, and don't bring that sister of yours along with you. This is to be work, not a social get-together.'

He strode away, and Averil realised she had been slow-witted. Though she had no qualms about going to his flat alone, since he had made it so very plain that his interest in her was not amorous, she could have pretended to have them, he had asked her if she had any objection. Now she was committed and she could only trust that her unruly heart would behave itself. Probably Philip would do nothing more than feed her cues, and as long as he did not touch her she could so immerse herself in her role that she would forget her personal involvement.

When they left the theatre Cecily asked her if she would mind being left alone that evening as she had accepted a date with McAllister, the stage manager. About to say she also had a date, Averil checked herself. Cecily was too ready to attach romantic motives to Philip's actions. Instead she told her she would take the opportunity to put in some concentrated study of her lines, which was in a sense true.

'Always so dedicated,' Cecily said. 'Don't you ever relax, Avvy?'

'I can't until after the first night,' Averil declared.

Cecily changed into a daring evening gown that she had recently bought, with practically no back, and pirouetted in front of the mirror in their room, asking with unwonted diffidence:

'I look more than not quite eighteen, don't I, darling?'

'At least twenty-five,' Averil told her, laughing. 'I suppose McAllister doesn't want to be accused of cradle-snatching.'

Cecily smiled. 'Well, I expect he looks down upon teenagers, being so mature himself, but I like grown-up men. By the way, his name's Ian.'

'Enjoy yourself.' Averil kissed her. 'What is it? Dinner?'

'And a show. Goodness, is that the time? I must fly!' She picked up her coat. 'I wish I had an evening wrap. That'll be my next extravagance.'

'You'll only have Sunday evenings free once the play starts, and then we'll be going to Elmsford.'

'You will,' Cecily corrected her. 'I'm not sure I want to go home every weekend. Nor is it necessary. You'll have John.'

She departed, leaving Averil with a sense of depression. She depended more upon her sister than she admitted, and Cecily was moving away from her. True, she had John, and once they were married Cecily would be outside her life, and she doubted if her sister would ever come back to live in Elmsford. She did not like changes, but she recognised that they were inevitable, and she began to wonder if she herself would be the same person when *Romeo and Juliet* was over.

Mrs Reubens provided early supper for Averil when she told her she had to go out, but she did not tell Rachel where she was going, for she, like Cecily, was too fond of looking for romantic connotations, when she was merely about to put in several hours' hard work. Because of that, and remembering Philip's quip about a social get-together, she did not put on a dress, but wore her usual trousers and tank top with a short cream jacket, for the evening had turned chilly.

She set forth with some curiosity to find Philip's abode.

CHAPTER SIX

PHILIP lived in an expensive service flat in Mayfair, and a manservant opened the door to Averil's timid ring. His appearance gave her a faint shock, as did the opulent furnishings of the flat. She knew from the address that Philip maintained some style, but she had not expected a butler, valet or whatever he termed himself.

The room into which he showed her was spacious with a thick blue carpet covering the floor, and blue velvet curtains at the tall windows. Two armchairs and a wide settee also covered in blue were placed before the electric stove and a piano stood in one corner. The walls were cream with a couple of ultra-modern paintings giving a note of vivid colour, there was also a bookcase, a desk and several occasional tables, but no knick-knacks nor ornaments, no photographs or vases of flowers. The room was completely impersonal.

Philip came out of an inner door which probably led into his bedroom, as Averil stood looking about her. He was wearing black dress trousers which suggested he had been dressing to go out, but instead of coat and vest, he had put on a heavy silk Russian blouse with a mandarin collar. The garment made him look slightly barbaric.

'The young lady, sir,' the man said deferentially from the doorway.

'Good evening, Averil.' Philip's greeting was off-hand. 'Walker, bring us some drinks and then you can go off duty. I'm going out myself later on, so I shan't want anything more tonight.'

'Very good, sir.'

Walker withdrew and Philip indicated one of the chairs with a movement of his head.

'Sit down, child, and make yourself at home. Find the way all right?'

'Oh, yes, I'm beginning to know London.' She sank down into the luxurious depths of the armchair in which she felt lost.

The windows were open to the fading daylight, but Philip drew the curtains over them and switched on the light.

'More private,' he said with a lopsided smile.

Walker returned with a silver tray on which were bottles of whisky, sherry, Martini, soda water syphon and appropriate glasses. He set it down on a table and stood to attention.

'I may go now, sir?'

Philip nodded and as the man withdrew, Philip noticed the amusement in Averil's eyes.

'Didn't expect to encounter Jeeves, did you?' he enquired, interpreting its cause correctly. 'Walker's invaluable, he does everything, including cooking, if I should require a meal, though most of our food is sent up. What will you have?' He moved to the tray.

'Nothing, thank you.' Averil suddenly realised that she was completely alone with Philip in a setting which looked most unsuitable for a rehearsal.

'Nonsense, a drink will help you to relax,' he declared, and poured her out a mild sherry. He gave himself a stiff whisky, and Averil had the odd sensation that he was no more at ease with her than she felt with him, which was absurd, this was his home ground, so to speak, and she was the alien. Her eyes wandered round the room, noting how expensive were its furnishings, and catching her wondering expression, he explained:

'My father was a very wealthy man, and left me quite a fortune. Since he didn't like my chosen profession, he never gave me anything in his lifetime once I was grown-up. He hoped to drive me into entering his business. Could you see me sitting at a desk all day?'

'No, but I could imagine you directing a commercial empire.'

Philip laughed. 'I wasn't offered one. However, the old boy didn't cut me out of his will as I half expected, so now I can indulge my luxurious tastes.'

'Including Jeeves? But you don't have to work?'

He smiled wryly. 'By the time my father went, work had become a habit. I'd be lost without it. Hard work is the finest cure for—er—disappointment that there is.'

She looked at him in wide-eyed surprise. 'But you've got everything, Mr. Conway.'

'I missed out on the thing I wanted most,' he said shortly. 'Shall we make a start?' He took her glass from her and indicated the settee. 'Lie down on that, there's a good girl.' He grinned mischievously. 'Imagine it's your marriage bed.'

Feeling acutely self-conscious, Averil lay down on the settee as requested, while Philip ruffled through the pages of his script. 'Now for that controversial scene,' he went on. 'Remember, you've just awakened from a night of love knowing that your husband is a wanted man and must be away before daylight. But you can't bring yourself to face the grim reality, you're trying to kid yourself it's still night. Now, a soft sensuous reproach. "Wilt thou begone? It is not yet near day."'

Averil had the utmost difficulty in projecting herself into the play, distracted as she was by her surroundings and Philip's proximity. The soft sensuous tone was a complete failure. Philip compressed his lips and came to sit on the edge of the settee, pushing her knees back to give himself room. He was facing her, sitting sideways as she lay back on the cushions. His nearness disconcerted her and her pulses quickened. She said uncertainly, anxious to distract him:

'Why don't you play Romeo yourself? You'd be a lot better than Nigel.'

'Think so? Unfortunately I'm at least fifteen years too old. This is a play about ardent, passionate youth frustrated by the stupid feuds and prejudices of its elders, as I think I've said before. Now come on, say that line again. The curtain goes up and we're discovered in each other's arms.'

He leaned over her, encircling her with one arm, and dropped his head upon her breast. The weight of it upon her caused her heart to beat so fast that she was sure he must be aware of it. His thick blond hair was soft under her chin. It was with relief that she felt him slowly withdraw himself.

'Now.'

'Wilt thou begone?' It did not sound like her own voice.

He sat up abruptly.

'You sound as if I were leaving after a vicarage tea party, not a night of love. Okay, carry on, we'll come back to it.'

Romeo must go, for if he is found in Verona after daybreak he will be executed for causing Tybalt's death, but Juliet continues to protest that he need not go yet. Finally, (in Philip's version) he throws himself back beside her, declaring he will risk discovery and stay if that is her wish. At that point Philip flung himself upon Averil with desperate abandon, but instead of responding, she went rigid.

106

'For God's sake let yourself go, girl,' he growled in her ear. 'Relax. You're a young girl experiencing the intensity of her first passion.'

Then suddenly his arms tightened and he was kissing her savagely, lips, eyelids, throat, and lips again. Averil felt a surge of emotion rise up and overwhelm her, setting her alight. Her body became fluid beneath his, her lips parted as she returned his kisses, her arms clasped his neck. Romeo—Philip, it was all one, it was, as he had said, she was submerged in the flood of her first experience of passion. John had been quite incapable of so moving her; actually he had never tired, nor had she had any inkling that love could be so devastating.

Abruptly Philip disentangled himself and stood up, while Averil lay gazing up at him, her dark eyes expressing all that she had wanted to conceal. Philip was breathing quickly and his eyes were alight with blue flame.

'That ... that wasn't acting,' he accused her unsteadily.

As the full realisation of what had occurred swept over her, Averil struggled up into a sitting position, and covered her face with her hands. She had utterly betrayed herself.

Philip poured himself another drink, swallowed it quickly and returned to loom over her, saying calmly:

'Though I want you to express emotion, you must never lose control of yourself.'

She flinched from the implied rebuke, and a fury of resentment shook her, at his coldness.

'It was your fault,' she flung at him, dropping her hands. 'You may be able to turn your feelings off and on like a tap, but I can't, because they're genuine. I ... I can't pretend any more.'

He looked at her oddly. 'Haven't you ever been

kissed before? What's your John been about?'

'John would never behave like you did. He ... respects me.'

Philip laughed scornfully. 'That won't get him far. I rather suspected he was a cold fish, but perhaps you don't give him the encouragement you gave me?'

Averil's face flamed at what seemed to her to be a cruel taunt. She turned her head away, her lips trembling.

'I didn't want to ... to love you,' she murmured, fighting for control. 'I tried to be true to John.' Her voice rose in a cry of despair, as she faced him. 'Oh, why did you have to come into my life, disrupting it? I was so happy before I met you, but you've spoilt everything.'

Her face puckered and she burst into a storm of tears, hiding her face against the arm of the settee.

Philip moodily regarded her shaking shoulders, covered by the tangled strands of her hair. An uncharacteristic look of compassion crossed his face, to be succeeded by a frown.

'Come,' he said kindly. 'This won't do. There's nothing to cry about.'

Her voice came muffled by her sobs: 'I'm so ashamed, but I couldn't help it. It's routine with you, isn't it? You expect your leading ladies to succumb to your practised wiles.'

'Don't talk like a novelette,' he told her impatiently. 'I haven't practised any wiles upon you. Stop blubbering like a baby, and pull yourself together. I'm not impressed by feminine tears.'

Averil remembered that he was notorious for making his actresses weep. So far he had handled her gently, but now she was receiving the full treatment. He seemed determined to ignore her exposure of her inmost feelings, but though that might salve her pride it gave her chill comfort. It was nothing to him if he broke her heart. What had seemed to her to be a momentous revelation he treated with indifference, but she was being naïvely childish to expect any other reaction. She pushed her hair back from her tear-stained face and fumbled in her pocket for a hand-kerchief, only to find that she had come out without one. Sniffing, she asked:

'Have you a tissue? I've mislaid my hanky.'

He muttered an imprecation, strode into the bed-room and returned with a folded silk handkerchief, which he pushed into her hand. Averil sat up, mop-ping her face with it, while Philip lit a cigarette.

'I must look a sight,' she murmured. He smoked in silence. 'I'm sorry,' she went on. 'I don't often cry, but ... but...' Her voice died away, for what excuse could she offer?

He found one for her. 'You were over-stimulated,' he told her. 'You've had a lot of adjusting to do since you came to town.'

He came to stand behind the settee, looking over its back at her with an enigmatical expression, his eyes narrowed against the smoke from his cigarette.

'Might one ask a personal question?'

'Certainly.' She wondered what was coming now, she had already stripped herself for his benefit, what fur-ther confession could he desire.

'Do you still intend to marry John Woods?'

The enquiry was so unexpected that she stared up at him blankly out of bewildered dark eyes.

'But of course.'

'In view of what you've just betrayed, do you con-sider that is being quite honest?'

'Because I'm a fool that's no reason to make John unhappy,' she declared vehemently.

'Would he be happy knowing your heart belonged

elsewhere?'

'He must never know that.'

'You wouldn't be able to deceive him, you're as transparent as glass, Averil.'

'To you, perhaps,' she returned, 'but dear John isn't so perspicacious. Anyway, as you know very well, all girls get crushes. I . . . I shall get over it.' She bit her lip to still its trembling.

'Then there's no need to make such heavy weather of it.' He turned away to stub out his cigarette, his lip curling cynically. 'You're not the first actress I've directed to be taken that way.'

'I didn't suppose I was,' she retorted with a flash of spirit. 'You thrive on broken hearts, don't you?'

'Far from it, I find the intrusion of personal involvement very tiresome.' He looked at her out of the corner of his eyes. 'However, in the present situation it may have its advantages.'

'Meaning it'll improve my performance?'

He grinned. 'You need experience, and you were living your part very effectively. Have a drink, it'll help you pull yourself together.'

She shook her head. 'I want to go home.'

It was a cry from her heart and she did not mean back to Mrs. Reubens. She wanted to return to the safety and security of Elmsford, away from these new and complicated emotions that were shattering her peace.

'But we haven't finished the scene,' he objected.

'I can't possibly do any more of that,' she cried desperately. 'Mr. Conway, I can't continue with this play. I must go back to my home, and to John.'

'Impossible,' he said bluntly. 'I won't let you.'

'Oh, please! I'll never be able to do the part as you want it played and . . . and the whole situation is too humiliating.'

'Rubbish, you're indulging in self-dramatisation,' he said coldly. 'Your situation is quite ordinary. Young girls frequently imagine they're in love with their boss, father confessor or what have you. It would have been more suitable if you'd fixed your affections upon your Romeo, but since you haven't, that's no reason for throwing up your part, merely because I succeeded in getting the reaction I wanted from you.'

She shivered; he was so calculating and cruel, for he had deliberately awoken her emotions to serve his own ends. She had tried to make light of them, but she knew what she felt for him went much deeper than a mere crush, she could not continue in close contact with him enduring his contempt.

Fretting the handkerchief with nervous fingers, she said:

'Seriously, Mr. Conway, you made a big mistake when you engaged me to play Juliet. I don't belong to your world, the cast including Nigel despise me. I don't think I'm fitted for a stage career.' She sighed. 'A pity you transplanted me!'

'You'd have grown beyond your environment without my help,' he told her quietly. 'You're a late developer, Averil, people of great potential often are, and sooner or later you would have needed wider horizons. In short, you had to grow up.'

Such glib reasoning, and so meaningless. She closed her eyes. 'But not like this,' she protested. 'You've heard of forced plants, Mr. Conway, that's what you're trying to do to me. You're forcing my growth, and it's ... painful.'

Philip studied her for some moments in silence, noting the length of her lashes upon her youthfully rounded cheeks, the droop of her lips, the still childish curves of her body crouched in the corner of the big settee. Innocent and vulnerable, she was totally unsuited to the life into which he had thrust her, unless she had a champion to fight her battles for her. He began to pace the room, his head bowed in thought, with light noiseless footsteps, like some feline animal in a cage. Averil remained still, collecting her strength, for she knew she had not yet won her release and she was determined to go.

Philip came to a halt beside her. 'Possibly I can make amends,' he told her.

Without opening her eyes she shook her head.

'There's nothing you can do. It's too late.'

'Nonsense, your life is only just beginning. Your Juliet will be a success, and if you stay with me there'll be other triumphs.'

'I don't want them.' She opened her eyes and gazed beyond him at the opulent furnishings of the room. They would be barren triumphs without his love, and his continued presence would give her more pain than pleasure. 'The further I go, the greater will be the envy and spite I'll encounter,' she went on. 'I don't like your professional stage.'

'But I'll always be there to shield and protect you.'

'With your cold looks and your acid tongue,' she said bitterly.

'A director has to be able to control his cast, and I've been patient with you.'

'Until now.' She moved restlessly. 'It's no good, Mr. Conway...'

He interrupted quickly, 'Why have you ceased to call me Philip?'

'It was presumptuous.' She gripped her hands together, as he started to protest. 'Between you and me there's a great gulf, Mr. Conway, we view life from totally different angles, and after tonight we'll go our several ways, for I've decided I shall break my contract and go home.'

'We shall sue you.'

She smiled wanly. 'Why bother? Gemma Knowles is waiting to take my place. Everyone says she ought to be playing Juliet and it's only your cussedness that won't let her. Give her the part and then we'll all be satisfied.'

'We shall not all be satisfied. Gemma Knowles isn't my idea of Juliet and I don't admire her work.'

'Then you're in the minority. The others don't admire mine.' She raised her eyes to his face, full of desperate appeal. 'Please, Philip, let me go home.'

'No.' The monosyllable was curt and clipped. He walked away from her, his head bent in thought, while she wondered what further arguments she could muster to make him release her. He seemed to come to some decision, for he moved back towards her purposefully, to again take his stance behind the settee, and putting his hands upon the back of it, leaned forward to look into her face.

'Averil, will you marry me?'

'What?' She stared up at him in blank astonishment, but there was no gleam in his eyes and his face was still and quiet. 'Is this a joke?' she asked doubtfully.

'I'm perfectly serious.' He straightened himself. 'And I would ask you to think seriously about it. As I told you, I'm comfortably off, I can give you anything within reason that you want. All I ask of you is that you will continue to act under my direction.'

'Ah!' She drew a long breath. She had underestimated him. He had insisted upon her engagement for Juliet and for her to walk out on him would be a blow to his arrogant pride. To justify his action to his company he must make her a success, and to keep her he was even prepared to offer her marriage, but such an idea was completely crazy.

'We needn't do anything so drastic,' she told him quietly. 'If you want to save your face, you've only got to admit I've disappointed you and dismiss me for incompetence.'

'What rubbish are you talking now?' he demanded. 'Why should I need to save my face, and I'm not disappointed in you.' He sat down beside her and took her hands in his. 'I've great plans for you, Averil, a modern part lined up for you after Juliet. You may be approached by a television company, but I don't want you to try that medium yet, until I've established you.' He glanced at her downcast face, but she was completely unresponsive. 'Nobody with your talent could really want to bury herself in a place like Elmsford,' he went on persuasively. 'That's cowardice, because you're scared, and you are like a fawn in the jungle among my unscrupulous colleagues, but if you'll let me protect and guide you on your upward climb, you needn't be afraid of anything or anyone. I'll smooth the path for you, little one, if only you'll entrust yourself to me.'

The low vibrant voice was acting like a spell upon her, the clasp of his fingers drawing resistance out of her. She said weakly:

'My career seems to mean more to you than it does to me, but it's not the right reason for marriage.'

He flashed her a wicked, glinting look.

'There's a better one, isn't there? Which you've just confessed. God knows I'm too old a mate for you, but feeling as you do, perhaps you'll overlook the greying hair.'

She tried to pull her hands away. 'You haven't a grey hair on your head, and you'll never let me forget I'm a fool.'

'Delightful folly, and it's my trump card, which I mean to play for all it's worth. Come, Averil, your

114

heart and your career are staked against ... what?'

'Your indifference,' she said very low.

'I can't be indifferent to my leading lady.'

Exactly; he could not separate the girl from the actress, nor did she need a protector, for she did not want a career.

'I'm not free,' she reminded him. 'I'm engaged to John.'

'Break it off, it means nothing to you.'

'I don't admit that,' she told him, though she feared it was true. 'And it means something to him.'

'He'll have his car to console him.'

A sudden suspicion darted into her mind.

'Philip, was it you who lent him the money to get it?'

He released her hands and leaned back on the settee.

'Now why should you think that?' he parried.

'Somebody did, and he would never tell me who. I believe it was you.' She looked at him accusingly.

Philip smiled cynically. 'It certainly overcame his opposition.'

Averil sprang to her feet. The revelation was repugnant to her. That John could have bartered her future for a car was a painful thought.

'So the loan for the car was a sort of bribe?' she demanded indignantly.

'You might say that.' He shrugged his shoulders. 'And as I've bought him off once, I daresay the process can be repeated.'

'What do you mean?'

The blue eyes met her angry dark ones with cool effrontery.

'That he could be compensated for your loss.'

Averil flushed stormily. 'Oh, you!' she exclaimed. 'You think money can solve everything.'

'It usually can.'

'Not in this case. John loves me, he isn't mercenary, but you couldn't understand that. He's not like you.'

'Not in the least,' he agreed. 'Are you sure your faith in him is justified?'

Averil had an uncomfortable mental flashback to a redhaired green-clad girl running down the stairs at Colchester station, and Cecily's remarks concerning her, but Clarice was only a casual acquaintance, she assured herself, John was too honest to deceive her; it was herself who was the unfaithful one.

'You're judging him by yourself,' she said scornfully. 'But I know him better than you do, and that's what makes me feel so awful. I just can't let him down.'

'Perhaps you'll change your mind,' Philip returned imperturbably. When *Romeo and Juliet* is a success.'

Averil jumped at the loophole he offered. 'Until we know it is nothing can be resolved,' she said decidedly.

'Oh, yes, it can.' He sprang to his feet and held out his arms. 'Come to me, sweetheart, I'll soon dispel your doubts.'

Averil backed away from him as he advanced upon her, his eyes alight. Once he had her in his arms she knew she would be utterly defeated, clay in the potter's hand. She drew herself up, crossing her arms over her breast, and faced him with quiet dignity. Something in her face checked him, he stopped and his arms fell to his sides.

'Please don't try to rush me, Philip,' she appealed to him. 'This a very serious matter, affecting three lives. I need time to think.'

He smiled satirically. 'You're growing up too fast, Averil, but at least you've stopped calling me Mr. Conway.'

Avery looked at him wistfully. If only he cared less about her career and more about her feelings! His interest in her lay wholly in her potentialities as an actress, and the girl, Averil Avon, came a very poor second. Had he loved her, she could not have hesitated, John notwithstanding, but it was power he desired, not love, it was her talent in which he was interested, not her person. If she had the success he prophesied, he would be the man who discovered and launched Averil Avon, and he meant to keep the new star under his domination. Moreover, once she was bound to him he would ensure that she could never escape back into peaceful nonentity at Elmsford. She had said her marriage to John would be a partnership, but Philip would make her into his slave. Yet even while the notion occurred to her, she knew it would be sweet bondage. Her pliable nature needed direction, a strong arm upon which to lean, she had no yearnings towards independence or asserting her rights. Her heart was urging her to take what he offered and surrender to his embrace whatever was motivating him, and that started another train of thought.

'I suppose you don't want a real marriage?' she asked ingenuously. 'I mean, if you only want to protect me...'

'Of course I want a real marriage,' he broke in brusquely. 'It's about time I got me a wife. Look at this,' he waved an arm indicating the flat. 'It's dead and simply crying out for a woman's touch.'

'Yet you've never thought of marrying before?'

His face darkened. 'We won't probe into my past life if you don't mind, my dear. It doesn't affect you. I can't offer you a boy's first passion, but I'll do my best to make you happy.'

'Thank you,' she murmured mechanically, while again she was intuitively aware that Philip had once loved and lost. She blurted out:

'Was she very beautiful?'

'Who?'

'Your first passion.'

He laughed. 'Of course, I'm susceptible to beauty.' His face hardened to stone and a brooding look came into his eyes. 'But I learned that beauty, as the saying is, was only skin deep.'

'I'm not beautiful,' Averil said despondently.

'You look it now and then and you've more important qualities—the freshness and guilelessness of youth and transparent honesty. You'd never let a man down.'

Her eyes widened in horror and her hand flew to her mouth.

'But I'd be letting John down.'

He made a wry face. 'It's only a boy-and-girl affair.'

'You want to make light of it to suit yourself.'

He said seriously: 'There's a vast difference between jilting a man because you find you no longer love him, then it's the only right course, and jilting a man you love because you've found a richer one.'

'Oh dear, but that's just how John would see it. You're better off than he is.'

'I'm not really interested in John Wood's reactions, only in yours.'

'And my success. But first we must be sure I am a success. You'll have to wait until after the first night before I can make up my mind.'

'Then you'll go on with the play?'

'I suppose I must,' she said wearily.

He came up to her and placed masterful hands upon her shoulders.

'You're not going to try to run away or do anything silly?'

She quivered under his hands. 'No, Philip, I promise you I'll go through with it.'

'Good girl, and I don't know what excuse you could

offer to John for backing out.'

'Oh, I could find plenty, and what would he say if I tell him you've proposed?'

Philip laughed. 'He wouldn't believe it. He'd say your innocence misunderstood my intentions and seduction is an occupational risk for actresses.'

'That doesn't sound like John,' she said uncertainly, wondering if she had misunderstood his intentions.

'John is growing up too and has a biased view of the stage and all professionals.' He looked down into her pale face with a quizzical smile. 'But you can trust me, my sweet, I'd never betray your innocence.'

Suddenly she knew that she could. Whatever his reputation was, however many affairs he had had, he would treat her honourably.

'Even if I refuse your offer?' she asked probingly.

'I'll take your refusal like a man, but you won't, will you, Averil?'

'I don't know,' she faltered distractedly, disturbed by the penetrating gaze. 'And I may be a flop.'

He drew her against himself and gently kissed her brow.

'You won't be, and I'll not press you until after the first night. After that beware, I'll not give you up without a fight.' Noticing her pallor, he went on: 'You look tired, have a rest tomorrow. Gemma can stand in for you, and it's about time I put her through it. After all she'll have to play it if you're ill, which God forbid.'

Averil drew away from him, subtly repelled by the menacing note in his voice when he spoke of putting Gemma through it. Disliking the girl, he would enjoy making her cringe.

'Poor Gemma,' she said. 'You're unkind.'

'She can take it, I don't have to handle her with kid gloves on like I do you.'

'Because I can't?'

He smiled mockingly. 'You wept.'

The hot colour stained her face. 'That was for another reason.'

'Blush like that and I won't be able to let you go,' he said harshly. He glanced at his watch. 'Heavens, is that the time? Excuse me, I must ring for a taxi.'

He went to the telephone and when he had given his order, she picked up her bag and jacket preparatory to leaving.

'You're going out, and I'm afraid I've made you late,' she said conventionally. 'I'll say goodnight.'

'Wait a minute. I have to go to an evening party, a deadly bore, but there'll be people there I want to meet. If you'll excuse me while I finish dressing, I'll give you a lift. I don't use my car much in town.'

'Oh, don't bother, I can walk,' she said, moving towards the door.

'You'll do no such thing at this hour. Will you promise to stay put until I'm ready, or must I tie you to my bedpost?'

'I promise,' she cried, laughing, and sat down on the settee.

But when the bedroom door closed behind him, her amusement faded. If she gave her life into Philip's hands she would soon have no will left, but neither would she have to make her own decisions. He would push her relentlessly up the ladder of fame whether she wished it or not, for he possessed all the ambition that she lacked, but she would not mind so long as he was there to support her. How very different her future would be with him from the one she had envisaged with John, and he might not want the family that she and John planned. But nothing really weighed against the tremendous fact that Philip had offered to marry her. It was the fulfilment of her wildest dreams, and though she hated the thought of hurting John, it would be unfair, as Philip had implied, to marry him when her heart was given to another. Everything depended upon her success, for if she failed to put Juliet across, she was certain Philip would no longer want her.

He came back resplendent in his dress clothes and they went down together to the waiting taxi. Averil caught sight of herself in the mirror in the lift, a pale uninteresting-looking girl, she thought, with her long straight hair, beside the distinguished-looking man in his elegant black and white. They made an incongruous pair.

CHAPTER SEVEN

AVERIL did not go to Elmsford the following weekend. She received a letter from John saying he would unfortunately be tied up that Saturday, though he did not specify how. He pointed out that she could get a bus from Colchester to the village, but since that entailed a long and tedious journey along a roundabout route, Averil decided to remain in town, although she would not be able to go to Elmsford for some time, for the next weekend, the one before the opening night, would be too hectic to permit her to leave.

She was not sorry to have an excuse not to see John, for in the circumstances it would be a little difficult to face him. Once the first night was over, and she knew how her Juliet had been received, she would have to make up her mind what she was going to do. If she failed, she did not think Philip would renew his offer, but it would be hardly fair to John to use him as an alternative, nor could she contemplate marrying him when her heart was given elsewhere. John had promised to bring her parents up with him to attend her debut, and she wrote that she would be seeing him then, though they were unlikely to have any time alone together.

In the meantime she had little leisure to think about her personal problems amid the rush of costume fittings, photographing, semi-dress rehearsals, and the ever-mounting tension in the theatre as the opening night approached. She never saw Philip alone, and while he directed he was aloof and sarcastic as usual, with the difference that he no longer spared her the edge of his tongue. He was working under considerable pressure with the responsibility for the play's success upon his shoulders, and was unable to completely control his irritability. Realising the strain he was enduring, Averil found she was able to sustain his criticisms, and at least the company could not imply that she was being treated with favouritism.

As she was not going home, Rosamund Brent asked her to spend Sunday with her at her house by the river, and since Cecily had her own arrangements, Averil accepted gratefully, for she liked the elderly actress.

In spite of her advancing years, Rosamund was strong as a horse, and commuted between her riverside home and the theatre, driving her mini to the station, where she parked it until her return at night. She met Averil with it on the Sunday morning, with her two grandchildren, Ivor and Tess, crammed into the back seat.

'They're spending the end of the holidays with me', she explained, 'and insisted upon coming along for the ride. I hope you don't mind. I won't let them bother you.'

'I'm sure I shan't find them a bother,' Averil said, turning to smile at the two youthful faces behind her. They were both blue-eyed and dark-haired, Tess was eight and Ivor a year younger.

'Mummy and Daddy are in Spain,' Tess informed her, 'making a simply super film. I wish we could go to Spain, but we have to go to a horrid old boarding school.'

'Oh, come, Tess, you know you like school,' her grandmother protested. 'And your parents can't look after you properly while they're working.' She edged her small car past a bus. 'Darned great things, take up all the road,' she grumbled. 'We're a theatrical family, as you may have surmised. My daughter married a film director, but it's always a bit rough on the kids when they have to go away on location. I can't look after them all the time. As it is I have to leave them in the evening, but I've a very reliable housekeeper who's very good with them provided she doesn't have too much of them.'

'Whitey says she couldn't have too much of us,' Ivor objected.

'We won't put her to the test,' Rosamund laughed. 'Here we are, Riverside House,' as she drew up in front of a charming house. 'The children will take you on to the lawn while I put the car away, and you can lounge there all day since it's so warm and sunny and relax.'

The children escorted Averil through the house and out on to a wide spread of mown grass reaching to the river. Trees and bushes divided it from the neighbours' gardens and gave it privacy. Tess gravely indicated the assorted collection of canvas chairs set out on it, asking her which she would prefer, and whether she would like a glass of lemonade, and when she said she would, scampered away to fetch it for her. Averil slipped off the thin jacket she was wearing over a sleeveless linen dress, and stretched her long limbs gratefully on a low lounger to enjoy the sun. If she had a boy and a girl like Tess and Ivor, she would not want to have to go off to Spain leaving them in a boarding school, but then she was not a dedicated artiste.

They had lunch in the cool dining room, a sunblind outside the window keeping out the sun. 'Whitey', otherwise the reliable housekeeper, Mrs. White, had prepared it, and joined them at table. She was a pleasant, homely woman, who obviously adored the children. Afterwards they went back to the lawn, and while Rosamund dozed, Ivor wandered down to the river, paddling among the reeds that fringed it and getting himself daubed with mud, which did not matter as he was wearing abbreviated shorts. Tess sat on the grass beside Averil, clad in a minuscule bikini, displaying for her benefit her cardboard theatre, a small model fitted with wings, flies and curtain. She used chessmen for her characters, and insisted that Averil must listen to her drama, which she made up as she went along. She mimicked the voices of each player, dulcet for her hero and heroine, gruff for her 'heavy' man, and squeaky for her comics. Averil was amazed at her invention and the variety of her vocal tones.

'No question but she'll follow the family tradition,' Rosamund Brent murmured sleepily. 'But I don't know about Ivor, he's a fancy for the sea. Hasn't drowned himself yet, has he?'

'He seems all right, a bit muddy. Can he swim?'

'Like a fish.'

Tea was brought out to them by Mrs. White, but she did not stay with them, and while Mrs. Brent was pouring out the first cupfuls, Tess gave a sudden ecstatic squeal and sprang up, scattering her chessmen far and wide, to race across the grass to greet the slim, elegant figure coming out of the house.

'Uncle Pip! Uncle Pip! Granny, Uncle Pip's come!' she shouted.

He was casually dressed in flannels and an open shirt, the sunlight finding golden lights in his fair hair. He came towards them sauntering over the turf, with Tess clinging to his arm.

'I thought I might be lucky,' he remarked with his eyes on the pot, 'if I dropped in at this hour.'

Averil's heart had given a lurch at the sight of him. She straightened herself in her seat, and pushed back her heavy hair.

'Your timing is excellent,' Mrs. Brent agreed. 'Tess, run and ask Mrs. White for another cup.'

Philip dropped into a spare canvas chair beside Averil's lounger, and smiled at her, a warm friendly smile without a hint of sarcasm.

'Not gone to Elmsford this weekend?' he enquired.

'No, John couldn't meet me and it's too much of a fag by bus. Mrs. Brent kindly took pity on me,' she said with some constraint, for she knew what he had expected her to say to John. At first she had thought he had come in search of her, but obviously he had not known she was there.

'Philip often drops in on Sundays if he's this way,' Mrs. Brent told her, as Tess returned with the cup. 'Especially if he knows the children are here.'

Tess knelt beside him on the grass, and he absently rumpled her hair.

'I've a weakness for juveniles,' he remarked, with a sly glance at Averil.

'When I'm grown up, I'm going to be Uncle Pip's leading lady,' Tess informed them.

'Maybe you will, if you work hard,' he returned,

'though by the time you're ready, I'll be getting a bit long in the tooth.'

'What's that mean?' the child demanded, looking anxiously at Philip's mouth. 'There's nothing wrong with your teeth, is there?'

'I hope not. It's an expression describing an affliction that affects horses and men of advancing years.'

'You mean you'll be old, like Granny?'

'I'm afraid so.'

'But Granny isn't awfully old, she still acts.'

'Yes, well, I expect I'll still be functioning when you want to make your debut. Meanwhile I've Averil to launch.'

Tess sighed. 'You're awfully lucky to be Juliet,' she said to Averil. 'Did you have to beg Uncle Pip awfully hard to let you be it?'

'Not exactly,' Averil said, aware of the amusement in Philip's eyes at this childish misconception. With an effort she made herself address him.

'I didn't know you had a niece and nephew.'

'He's only a courtesy uncle,' Mrs. Brent interposed, 'though I believe there is a very distant connection, third cousins or something.'

'I like curtsy uncles best,' said Tess, mispronouncing the word. She preferred Philip to her own kin.

Philip drank his tea, looking comfortably relaxed. Though he had given most of his attention to Tess, Averil was conscious that his eyes were frequently turned in her direction. That he was fond of children, or at least these children, had come as a surprise. Seeing him leaning back in his chair it was not difficult to imagine him as a family man, and the same thought occurred to their hostess, for she suddenly said:

'It's quite time you got married Philip, and had some domestic life apart from the theatre, you'd make an admirable father.'

'Would I?' His eyes sought Averil's. 'Perhaps I'm thinking of it.'

Averil avoided his look, nervously pleating her skirt. She knew he had done more than think of marriage, but up to now she had only viewed his proposal in connection with her career. That he might really need a home and family was a new idea to her.

Tess said jealously: 'I don't want you to marry, Uncle Pip. If you had a little girl of your own, you wouldn't have time for me.'

'I'd always have time for you,' he assured her, 'even if I had a dozen kids.' This time the look he gave Averil was definitely mischievous.

Ivor came back from the river followed by a large swan which appeared to know it was a family meal-time.

'Lohengrin wants his tea,' the boy announced, seizing a piece of bread and presenting it to his protégé.

'Really, Ivor, I wish you wouldn't encourage that bird,' his grandmother complained. 'No, not the plum cake. It's too good for swans. Go and ask Mrs. White for some crusts.'

Ivor departed, while the bird, planted firmly on its webbed feet, waved its snakelike head about belliger-ently, seeking further sustenance. Tess crept nearer to Philip.

'I don't like Lohengrin,' she confessed. 'He's so big.'

Philip put his arm round her. 'Are you often in-vaded?' he asked Mrs. Brent.

'Only when Ivor's here. The swans are quite smart enough to have learned that picnickers mean scraps,' Rosamund told him. 'They organise a sort of black-mail. Tess isn't the only one to be scared of them.'

Ivor came careering back with a bag of crusts and Mrs. Brent insisted that he lure Lohengrin back to the water with them.

'His pals are coming to join him.' She indicated several graceful white forms approaching the bank. 'We don't want a whole flock of them, and Tess is frightened of them.'

'Silly sissy,' Ivor said scornfully, but he persuaded his pet to return the way he had come and remained to distribute his largesse at the water's edge to the greedy birds. They made a decorative tableau, the boy's brown limbs and the great white birds, with the sparkling water behind them and the blue sky above. Averil watched them idly, enjoying the pleasant, peaceful scene, so that Philip's next words came as a shock.

'Did you know that Lord Raydon has been killed?'

'No! When? How?'

'It was given out on the news. It seems their camp was invaded by lions and one of them got him. Poor old Arthur, he wouldn't willingly have hurt a fly.'

'You knew him?' Mrs. Brent asked.

Philip's lip twisted sardonically. 'I did. We had—er—kindred tastes.'

Averil missed the implication. 'Oh, poor Lady Raydon!' she exclaimed, her thoughts having flown to her old friend.

'She'll hardly miss him, she saw him so seldom,' Philip observed cynically.

Averil looked at him reproachfully, thinking the crack was out of place.

'It's a dreadful thing to have happened,' she reproved him. 'Lady Raydon was coming to the first night and I was hoping to see her, but of course she can't now.'

Philip looked at her curiously. 'Has she contacted you since you've been in London?'

'No. I've a feeling I've displeased her somehow. She ... she cooled off when you engaged me, though I thought that was what she wanted.'

'Women are never consistent,' he observed drily, and yawned. 'Your garden is a delightful spot, Rosa, but if I stay here any longer I'll fall asleep, and I must be on my way.'

'Can't you stay for supper and take Averil back with you?' Mrs. Brent asked, and Tess chimed in:

'And see me in bed, Uncle Pip, and tell me a story.'

He shook his head. 'Sorry, Tess, even that delightful prospect can't tempt me from my duty. I want to try some lighting effects while the theatre is closed.' He stood up and stretched. 'Thank you, Rosa, for the tea, it's put new life into me.'

'Do you have to work on Sundays?' Rosamund asked.

'Yes, with the opening only two weeks off. See you tomorrow, Averil, on set. Poppet, come and see me off.'

He strode off with Tess again clinging to his hand to seek his car on the other side of the house. Averil was vaguely disappointed; he had not tried to speak to her alone, in fact he had treated her as a mere chance acquaintance. Perhaps the news about Lord Raydon had upset him, but she had never heard that they were close friends. She had understood his connection was with the wife, not the husband.

Mrs. Brent watching Philip disappear. She sighed and said:

'I wish he would get married and forget that old affair.'

'What affair?' Averil asked eagerly.

'He was jilted, you know, just before the wedding. The girl must have been a hussy, but he's stayed over faithful to his first love.'

This was the occurrence Averil had always suspected, that had caused him to become so cynical. Mrs. Brent went on:

'But that was ages ago. I had hoped that Gemma...' She shrugged her shoulders. 'She's tried hard enough to get him, but she's made no impact.'

Averil saw that it had not crossed Rosamund's mind that she herself might be in the running. Presumably Mrs. Brent considered her to be too young, and Philip's manner towards her had given no hint that he took a romantic interest in her. She was having difficulty in crediting that he had actually asked her to marry him. No one seeing him there that afternoon could possibly suspect that he was her suitor. Perhaps he was having second thoughts about it. He had been prompted by a chivalrous impulse to spare her feelings when she had so naïvely betrayed herself, though such an action was uncharacteristic of him. If he did bring the matter up again when the period of her proviso had expired, it could only be because he wanted to have sole control of her future. She looked towards the empty chair where he had sat with Tess at his feet. That was what she wanted, a garden, a home and children like Tess and Ivor, with Philip relaxed among them. That was her idea of marriage, but it was unlikely it could be fitted into the life he was mapping out for her.

She said hesitantly: 'Did you find having a family interfered with your acting, Mrs. Brent?'

'It would be better put the other way round,' Rosamund said, laughing. 'The family had the first priority. I gave up while the children were small. I have two sons beside a daughter and I only went back to the stage when they could do without me.'

Averil sighed. She saw no prospect of persuading Philip to put a potential family first, but she could no longer contemplate marrying John if her Juliet was a flop. There was no way back into her former life. As Philip had said she would, she had grown out of it. She wondered a little dismally what would become of her if Philip repudiated her.

Mrs. Brent looked at her kindly. 'You look sad, dear, are you distressed about the accident to your friend's husband?'

'I hardly knew Lord Raydon,' Averil told her, 'but I'm sorry for his wife and family.' She was guiltily aware that she had not been thinking about them at all.

Her invitation included supper, and at Tess's insistence, she helped to put the children to bed and much increased her popularity by telling them a story when they were settled in the room they shared. Ivor disdained a goodnight kiss, but Tess wreathed her arms about Averil's neck, murmuring:

'You're ever so nice; you must come again soon.'

Tucking in the sheet and looking down at the flower-like face on the pillow, Averil wondered how the child's mother could bear to go off to Spain leaving her behind.

Mrs. Brent called up to her saying more visitors had arrived, and going downstairs, she found Cecily and Ian McAllister in the sitting room. It turned out that Ian often called in at Riverside House on Sundays, and they had come to take Averil home. Rosamund insisted they both must stay for supper, and over the meal Averil gave Cecily Philip's news about Lord Raydon. Though her sister expressed sympathy for the widow, she too found him too remote to feel any personal regret.

'To think Robert is now Lord Raydon!' she remarked pensively.

'Who's Robert?' Ian demanded suspiciously.

Cecily dimpled. 'An admirer of mine.'

The stage manager's red whiskers seemed to bristle as he said belligerently: 'Of course I can't compete with a title.'

'Are you competing?' Cecily enquired, her eyes

sparkling.

'Robert's a schoolboy,' Averil interposed. 'She's only teasing you, Ian.'

'But schoolboys soon grow up, and he has got a pash on me,' Cecily persisted provocatively.

McAllister laughed. 'You need a man to handle you, my lass, not a lad.'

'Too true,' she simpered. 'Avvy and I like 'em well seasoned.'

Mrs. Brent turned a thoughtful eye upon Averil as if a new idea had occurred to her, and the girl hastily changed the subject to the play.

'It'll be a success,' Ian predicted. 'Philip's innovations have made sure of that. The substitution of a street brawl for the duel scene with Mercutio and Tybalt stabbed with flick knives instead of a rapier fight will cause a furore. The purists will call it blasphemy because he's even dared to alter a word or two in the text to fit his conceptions and the public will flock in to see what the row's about. I like the idea of having the last scene set in a chapel beyond the grave-yard with Juliet lying in state before the altar. The vault was always a bit implausible.'

'The play's terribly hackneyed,' Cecily observed. 'I'm glad he's managed to do something original with it.'

'Our Philip's always original,' Ian stated solemnly. 'And with a new unknown Juliet——' he grinned at Averil, 'the critics will have a busy night.'

'Averil'll be all right,' Cecily said quickly.

'I hope so,' Averil sighed.

'Don't worry,' Ian assured her. 'Philip's never made a mistake yet.'

McAllister was correct in his predictions. The conventional reviewers were so outraged by the liberties Philip had taken with tradition that they had little to say about anything else. The more avant-garde praised his courage, saying he had infused new life into old bones. Controversy raged and amidst it all individual performances were almost ignored. The critics were kind to Averil, a few noted that she lacked experience but stated that her sincerity and appealing charm made up for it, others remarked upon her considerable dramatic force, which was unusual in one so young. But the notices in the morning papers seemed a long way off when in a state of nervous trepidation Averil made ready on the opening night.

Philip had dressed his players in modern clothes with a psychedelic slant, using a great deal of black and white with occasional splashes of vivid colour. Romeo wore black and gold, Juliet white and silver with a long black wig of flowing hair. Averil's first dress was a long evening gown, the bodice trimmed with silver and a silver fillet on her head. Make-up and fright made her dark eyes look enormous.

She had flowers and telegrams from her family, John, Mrs. Reubens and Lady Raydon. Philip sent her a large bunch of roses. He came to inspect her when the quarter had been called and surveyed her critically.

'You'll do,' he said briefly.

She put out a trembling hand. 'Philip, I'm scared stiff.'

He took it in a reassuring clasp, and grinned.

'All the best artistes are sick with nerves beforehand, they aren't a lot of good if they aren't.' He pressed her fingers. 'You'll be all right once you get on stage.'

'I . . . I hope so.'

'I know so. Well, my child, my job is finished. When the curtain goes up tonight my responsibility ends and it's over to the stage manager.'

She saw that he was wearing an ordinary lounge

suit, not evening dress as she had expected, and she enquired anxiously:

'But you'll be in the theatre? It helps me to know that you're there.'

'Oh, I'll be around to see how it goes,' he returned, and suddenly she knew that he was nearly as nervous as she was. She recalled what McAllister had said about his production being controversial.

'Suppose the critics don't like it?' she queried.

'A lot of them won't, I know that,' he grinned impishly. 'That doesn't worry me if I can make 'em sit up. But they'll like you, so don't worry.'

He dropped her hand and glanced at the telegrams stuck round her mirror.

'So Gina sent you one,' he commented.

'Yes, wasn't it nice of her, when she must have so much else to think about.'

'Did she tell you she was coming? She's in front right now.'

'But she can't be!' Averil gasped, much shocked. 'Why, the funeral was only a few days ago.'

Mr. and Mrs. Avon had gone to it and had bemoaned the fact that their daughters were unable to attend it.

'Remnants of feudalism,' Cecily had said scornfully.

Averil knew that if she had been at Elmsford she would have gone with her fellow Thespians, who had sent a wreath to which she had subscribed, to show their sympathy for Lady Raydon. Moreover, her husband had been more successful as a zoologist than a peer, and his death had caused quite a stir in scientific circles. That his widow could so flout public opinion as to appear at a theatre so soon after his demise would cause a good deal of unfavourable comment and was uncharacteristic of Georgina, who normally respected appearances.

'She's hoping not to be noticed,' Philip told her. 'She's sitting in a box alone with a scarf over her head.' His eyes glinted. 'She forgets a veiled woman always excites male curiosity. She'll probably be taken for an oil sheikh's wife, except she's wearing no jewels.'

'You—have you spoken to her?' Averil asked eagerly, forgetting her coming ordeal.

'Not yet. She sent me a note explaining her presence. Apparently she just had to see her protégée make her debut.'

There was a satirical gleam in his eyes as if he did not believe that was her real motive, but Averil did not notice it.

'How sweet of her!' she exclaimed naïvely. 'I suppose I've been forgiven for whatever it was I did to offend her.'

Philip was about to speak, then checked himself and looked at her oddly. Finally he said flatly:

'She's asked me to give her my support, so I'll be watching the play from her box. You don't mind?'

'Mind? Why on earth should I mind? I'm glad she'll have an old friend with her to console her.'

Philip's expression became still more satirical.

'If she needs consolation,' he observed.

The tannoy announced 'Beginners, please,' recalling them to the imminence of curtain rise.

'This is it,' said Philip. 'At least her ladyship's appearance has diverted your attention from your nervous fears.'

'Is that why you told me?' she asked with a flash of gratitude.

'Partly. Now I must go. Good luck, little one, and bless you.'

The door closed behind him and Averil turned for a last glance into her mirror. The play had started and her hour of destiny was upon her.

The play ran with remarkably few hitches for a first night to its tragic conclusion. The last scene, where Juliet lay upon her bier, approached by several shallow steps through a wide archway from the darkened graveyard set on the forestage, was intensely moving in its poignancy. As Nigel's supposedly dead body lay beside her, Averil subconsciously transmuted the emotion she would feel if Philip were lost to her for ever into a sublime exposition of drama. Without Romeo-Philip she could not continue to exist, and as she stabbed herself with her lover's knife, she was almost exalted.

The Friar's explanation and the rather banal reconciliation of the two warring families had been cut as short as possible, but the words passed over Averil's head without meaning. It was not until the curtain fell and the applause rose like the thunder of a stormy sea breaking upon the beach that she returned to earth.

'Come on, girl, get up, you can't go to sleep there,' Ian roused her, and she stood up half dazed to take her place in the line to take the call.

Afterwards Nigel led her between the tabs, and they were recalled several times. Throughout the play she had been conscious of Philip's presence in the box at the end of the circle, though she had never once looked towards it. Some magnetic current had flowed between them, urging her on and giving her sustenance. Now she looked up hoping to win a smile of approval, and saw with an odd sense of shock that the box was untenanted. Naturally Lady Raydon would want to leave the theatre as unobtrusively as possible, and before it started to empty, and Philip would undertake to escort her to her car or taxi, whichever she had used. The acute feeling of deprivation that had assailed Averil when she discovered his absence had no foundation, but it continued with her on her way back to her dressing room, where she half expected to find him waiting for her, but only Maudie the dresser was there.

'Went off very well, miss, didn't it now?' the woman said.

'Yes, yes, it did,' Averil returned vaguely. Philip must still be seeing Lady Raydon off, but he would come before she was ready to leave the theatre and tell her he was well pleased with her.

She was in her wrap taking off her make-up when Mrs. Reubens burst into the room, followed by the Avons.

'Lovely, dearie,' Rachel declared, embracing her vigorously, heedless of grease and powder. 'I didn't know you had it in you. I found your mum and dad looking for you, and here they are.'

Averil smiled at her parents.

'It went off very well, didn't it?'

'You were wonderful, Avvy. I could hardly believe it was you,' Mrs. Avon declared tremulously. 'Though it's an awfully sad play. I liked that one you did in the spring much better.'

'Where's John?' Averil asked, noticing he was not there. She wondered what he had thought of her performance.

Mr. Avon cleared his throat. 'I'm sorry, Avvy, but John couldn't come.'

Averil stared at him with mingled astonishment and relief. She was feeling guilty about John; sooner or later she would have to break with him, though not tonight, but that he could have not come to her debut was unbelievable.

'How did you get here?' she murmured.

'By train, darling, and Mrs. ... your landlady has offered to put us up for the night,' her mother told her.

'So we won't have to rush off.'

'You're all coming back to my place to celebrate,' Mrs. Reubens announced. 'The girl deserves a bit of fêteing. Hurry up, dearie, and get dressed, and we'll be away. Cecily is bringing Ian McAllister to join us and he's gone to get some champagne.'

'Lovely,' Averil murmured automatically. What could have kept John away, and where was Philip?

'John isn't ill?' she asked.

'Not that I know of,' Mrs. Avon said angrily. 'It's too bad of him. You must have been counting upon seeing him and he should have been the first to congratulate you.'

'I'll survive,' Avril returned. 'After all, he doesn't like Shakespeare.'

John's neglect made little impact upon her, but where was Philip? Surely he would not leave the theatre without contacting her? If he came could she persuade him to join Mrs. Reubens' party? It would not be much of a celebration without him.

Her visitors left her to get dressed and while Maudie was helping her her ears were strained to catch the sound of Philip's voice in the passage, her nerves taut to anticipate his knock. He might have been delayed by his own friends, reporters, anybody, but surely he must come before she left.

She dallied as long as she could, until Cecily came rushing in full of excited impatience.

'Whatever's keeping you, Avvy? We're all waiting for you, and so are your fans, quite a crowd of them outside the stage door. Ian says we'd better go out through the front of the house to escape them or we'll be here all night. Unless you want the thrill of signing a hundred autographs?'

Averil looked appalled. 'Not tonight, I'm so tired.'

'Well then, come on. Ian's got two taxis waiting.'

'Just another five minutes,' Averil told her. 'Don't wait, I'll meet you by the box office.'

She did not want Cecily there if Philip did come. Her sister looked at her compassionately, noting her wan face.

'John's a skunk,' she said fiercely. 'No wonder you're upset. Come along, darling, I'm sure you've got everything. Oh dear,' she glanced at her bare wrist, 'I must have left my watch in my dressing room. Okay, meet you where you said.'

The theatre seemed empty when Averil finally stepped into the dimly lit passage outside her door. A few stage hands were wandering about, but that was all. She made her way to the pass door into the auditorium which led by the little room that was used as an office. The door was slightly ajar and the light was on, which was unusual, as at this hour it was normally locked. Averil halted, wondering if Philip were inside, possibly collecting some data he needed. A familiar voice came out to her from behind the half closed door, a voice she had not heard for some time.

'But, Philip darling, haven't you realised I'm free now? We can go back to where we left off. The boys are growing up, they don't really need me now, and I know you do. You still love me, don't you?'

A murmur from Philip that Averil could not catch, then Lady Raydon's clear concise tones:

'You needn't have any scruples now. At last I'm in a position to reward you for all your years of faithful devotion.'

Averil fled through the pass door and stumbled up the darkened gangway towards the entrance to the theatre. How could she have been so blind? So many things had pointed to an affair between Philip and Georgina, but she in her naïve innocence had failed to notice their implication. Not surprising that she had waited in vain for Philip to come to her, she had been far from his thoughts. Lady Raydon was reasserting her old influence over him, and she had been the first love he had never been able to forget. Now with her husband dead they would be able to be reunited.

CHAPTER EIGHT

ACCORDING to theatre tradition whatever catastrophe befalls the play must go on, and Averil had no excuse not to perform her part, though she would have been thankful never to have gone near the Regina again. For two nights she went on wrapped in a sort of numbed apathy and naturally her mood was reflected in her work. Prior to curtain rise on the third evening, she overheard Nigel talking to Gemma.

'That's the trouble with these amateurs,' he was saying. 'They give a good show, but they can't sustain it. It's one thing to star once in a way at Puddle in the Mud, but it needs professionalism to maintain the same standard night after night.'

'If she gets much worse, the management will be asking me to take over,' Gemma declared smugly.

'The sooner the better, for the sake of the play,' Nigel concurred.

Averil's pride was stimulated. That night her Juliet was even better than upon her first appearance. She managed to infuse into it some of the heartbreak from which she was suffering. For Philip had not visited the theatre since the opening night. As he had told her, his part in the production was completed. Finished also was his interest in Averil Avon. He had decided to forget that he had proposed to her, and in justice to him she had to admit that she had not received his offer with great enthusiasm. But at the time he had made it, Lady Raydon had not been available; now she was free the situation had changed and he was probably hoping that she would go back to John. Georgina's coolness towards herself was now explained. She had resented Philip's absorption in his new leading lady, believing that she still held him in thrall. She was of course the girl who had thrown him over to marry wealth and a title, and though Philip had been so bitter against her, he had never lost touch with her, as his visits to the Towers went to prove. Compared with her ladyship's still considerable beauty, her style and wealth, for doubtless her late husband had left her well provided for, Averil had no chance, for Philip had always considered her to be almost a child and her passion for him no more than an adolescent crush that would evaporate as she grew older. Even his ambitions for her seemed to have waned, and she recalled how he had once said he had lost the thing he wanted most. Now it was being offered to him, he would have no consideration for anything else.

On the Sunday following the first week—the play had opened on a Tuesday—Averil went home to Elmsford, Cecily preferring to stay in London, while John had agreed to meet her at Colchester. She need not be back in the theatre until the Monday night and she was anxious to see him, though what she was going to say to him she was not sure. She was back to square one, with the difference that she now knew the affection she had for him was not love. She had had no direct communication from him since he had failed to come to her debut. Her mother had negotiated the

141

travelling arrangements, and she wondered what excuses he would offer for his non-appearance. So far she had received none, and she knew her parents were furious with him, for his neglect. She felt no rancour herself, and if she did decide to break with him his behaviour offered a way out.

John met her on the platform with polite formality and she thought he was looking sheepish. When they were in the car, he made a lame attempt at explanation.

'I'm not my own master, Avvy, and I had to work late on that Tuesday over a very important deal that had been entrusted to me. I couldn't make your folk understand that it was impossible to get away, but you've always been reasonable. I'm sure you'll understand.'

'I understand that our relationship has deteriorated,' she said gently. 'You didn't want to come, did you?'

'Of course I did,' he declared vehemently. 'Even though Shakespeare isn't my cup of tea.' He laughed a little forcedly. 'A pity your bent wasn't musical comedy, I'd find that much more entertaining.'

'Unfortunately I can't sing,' she reminded him drily.

'I must congratulate you,' he went on, 'a little belatedly, I'm afraid. According to the papers you were a success.'

'You can skip all that,' Averil told him. 'It was a somewhat barren triumph.' As he looked at her questioningly, she added, 'You didn't want me to go, and I ought to have been stronger-minded. If we hadn't let ourselves be over-persuaded we wouldn't have been in this mess.'

'What do you mean—mess?'

'That I've found I don't love you, John, and I don't believe you love me.'

'Oh, rot!' he exclaimed. 'Just because I couldn't make your first night you've decided I don't love you!'

'Do you still love me, John?'

'Well, I...' He hesitated and she marked it. 'Of course I do.'

She looked searchingly at his profile. 'You're sure?'

He drew into a layby, killed the engine and turned to face her. His fair, boyish countenance was flushed and sulky, so like he used to look in their teenage days when she had said something to annoy him. She felt a revival of her old affection for him, which was so very different from the overwhelming love she had for Philip.

'You're going to tell me you've fallen for someone else,' he said angrily. 'Some glamorous actor type. That's it, isn't it? It's what I was afraid would happen.'

Averil had no intention of trying to deceive him, but if he still cared for her, she might be able to make him happy if not herself. It was not what she had meant to say at all, but her future looked so bleak and lonely, she would be grateful for any warmth he could infuse into her desolation.

'It's over,' she told him quietly. 'Just a flash in the pan, so if you still want me...'

'I'm not sure that I do now, some simpering actor's cast-off.'

She winced at his callous tone and said earnestly:

'It wasn't like that at all. I ... I found out there was someone else ... I ... I'd misunderstood him.'

'Yes, you always were a bit of a simpleton.' He sounded appeased. 'It would be easy to deceive you.'

She writhed inwardly at his contemptuous tone, knowing his observation was only too true.

'I'll be coming back to Elmsford when *Romeo* is

over,' she informed him calmly. 'Probably it won't run beyond Christmas, the theatre is only on a short lease ... what's the matter?'

For John had uttered an exclamation of dismay.

'You don't really mean to come back, do you?'

'Certainly I do. Mr. Moreton promised me my old job would be waiting for me if I wanted it, and I'm hoping you'll be understanding, John, and help me to forget ... all that's happened since I left home.' Her voice quivered and tears rose in her eyes, but she resolutely controlled herself. 'I shall do, of course, in time, and then perhaps we can start again...'

But he was not listening to her; he cut her short, saying:

'If you go back to old Moreton you'll only be earning a pittance.'

Surprised, she returned: 'It used to be enough.'

He tapped his fingers on the dashboard impatiently.

'It's not enough now. To be honest, Avvy, I still owe Conway a hell of a lot on this car. We'll need much more than you can earn in Elmsford to get out of debt.'

At last he had admitted who his debtor was.

'You shouldn't have bought the car if you couldn't pay for it,' Averil rebuked him, 'and I'm surprised you could bring yourself to borrow from P ... Mr. Conway of all people.'

'He was so persuasive, Avvy, said I really ought to have one, and among other things it would be necessary to collect you to and from town, for you wouldn't be happy if you couldn't get back home every week. So as it was mostly on your account that I got it, it's up to you to help me to pay for it.'

'But you've got a much better job now,' she pointed out, while she assimilated this sophistry. John would not have needed a lot of persuading to accept the loan, since he had hankered after a car for so long, but who had put Philip up to it? Certain remarks Cecily had let drop recurred to her. It must have been her sister. Together they had been too wily for John and herself, and when Philip wanted something, he could be very wily indeed.

'I have that,' John said proudly. 'But of course you can't appreciate what I've done, having shot up to stardom yourself, but it's incurred many more expenses. I have to dress better and entertain customers.' He glanced at her slyly. 'Since you've been a success you can easily get another star part. I didn't want you to go, I'll admit, but as you've made a start, it would be a great pity not to go on.'

'But we'd be separated,' Averil pointed out. 'John dear, I want to come home, to find peace ... and healing.'

Her eyes were full of anguished appeal, but he looked away from her at the traffic speeding up and down the road.

'Do you expect me to act as an adhesive plaster?' he demanded brutally. 'You haven't treated me very fairly, Averil, and if you really want me to forgive you, you'll have to do as I suggest.'

Stung, she enquired: 'By acting as your banker?'

He turned a dull red. 'We've always pooled our resources,' he muttered.

'That was when we were saving for a home together.'

'Aren't we doing that now?'

'With me in London and you running after Clarice?'

It was a bow drawn at venture, but she was pained by his mercenary point of view. In spite of his assurance, she did not believe that he loved her; she had desperately wanted some show of affection, and all he was concerned about was the loss of her salary. Material possessions were all that modern young people valued, she thought despairingly, and John had completely changed from the pleasant unassuming young man he used to be.

At mention of Clarice, his colour deepened.

'Who's been talking?' he demanded.

'No one, but I saw her that evening at Colchester.'

'When you were speeding back to your actor pal? Fair's fair, Avvy, if you can sidestep, why not me?' He chuckled reminiscently. 'She's a one, is Clarice, and smart. She knows how to dress, which you don't.' He glanced disparagingly at her trousers and sweater.

'You've told me that before,' she said wearily. 'I'm just too tired and unhappy to doll myself up. I don't think there's any point in going any further. I don't intend to go on acting, nor to play second fiddle to your Clarice, and you can take back your ring.'

She pulled it off her finger as she spoke.

'Oh, come off it, Avvy, don't be so touchy,' he demurred. 'Can't you take a little criticism? I'm not serious about Clarice, and you said you wouldn't mind if I took a girl out once in a while when you were away.'

'Rather more than once in a while, I fancy, and possibly she was the real reason why you didn't come to my opening night.' Averil was hitting out at random, but her suspicions had been fully aroused. 'Suppose you take me home now and I'll make some other arrangement for future visits.'

'But my debt to Conway?'

'You'll have to settle that as best you can. I daresay he'll be lenient; he should be, for he's manipulated you as he manipulates everyone else, to suit his own ends.'

'Including yourself?'

'Myself most of all.'

John started the car and drove the rest of the way in sulky silence. Since he had not taken the ring, Averil dropped it into the glove compartment. Feeling guilty about John, not wanting to hurt him, she had meant to offer him a relationship in which she had hoped the affection she had had for him could be blown up into something resembling love. She needed someone upon whom to lean, and since Philip had failed her, she had contemplated turning back to John. Now she realised that what had once been between them was quite dead, and could never be rekindled. There was no solace to be had from him, and she admitted to herself that she had been a little unfair to expect it. If he had loved her he might have been willing to sustain her, but it had become very obvious that he did not; that sort of unselfish love was rare and to want to comfort her was beyond his capacity. To be tolerated because she could help him to repay his debt to Philip while he dallied with Clarice in her absence was a humiliation too great to be contemplated.

Mrs. Avon did not seem surprised when she told her John would not be coming to tea.

'He's confessed about that redhead?' she asked. 'But don't be too hasty, darling, it may only be he was lonely with you gone.'

'So it's common knowledge,' Averil said slowly, 'but it wasn't only that. Ours was a boy-and-girl affair, the result of propinquity, but we're both growing into different people.'

As Philip had told her they would.

She dreaded to learn that Philip was staying at the Towers, but it turned out the place was shut up, the boys being at school and Lady Raydon away, nobody seemed to know where. She was with Philip, Averil decided, and they would be making plans to marry as soon as they decently could, and though Georgina was actually older than Philip, she was still young enough for it to be possible for her to have a child.

Averil yielded to a nostalgic urge to visit the little theatre, though this too was closed. Because of Lord Raydon's death the Thespians' autumn production had been cancelled, and the building had a deserted look. How very dense she had been not to realise even then that there had been something between those two. The two boys had sensed it and resented it. Adoring Lady Raydon with a schoolgirlish reverence, she had taken it for granted that she had married for love, and no unfaithful thought could ever occur to her. Yet she had divined almost at once that Philip had experienced an unhappy love affair, which had made him so cynical, but she had never connected the two, though she had been told they had played together in *Quality Street* before Lord Raydon came on the scene. Whether the knowledge would have made any difference to her, she could not say, except that it would have tumbled Georgina off her pedestal. She had not been free when Philip had become interested in Averil, and it was possible that if Lord Raydon were still studying gorillas in Africa Averil might by now be engaged to Philip. Probably she had been spared much heartbreak by the poor man's demise, for Philip would never have come to love her while Lady Raydon held his heart, and would have fretted against the bond that kept him from her when she became available. Standing outside the little theatre that had been the scene of so many happy triumphs, she recalled Philip resplendent in his uniform as Captain Brown, and was swept by an almost intolerable longing for his presence. Leaning against a tree bole, she wept.

A patter of quick footsteps warned her someone's approach, and hastily mopping her eyes, she kept her back to whoever it was, hoping the intruder would pass by.

'Averil Avon!' exclaimed Molly Smith, prancing towards her. 'What's the matter? Not crying, are you?'

'I ... I've got a fly in my eye.'

'Can I help you get it out?'

'No, thank you, it's gone now.'

'We've been hearing great things about you,' Molly went on cheerfully. 'I feel privileged to think I once acted with you. Our next show has been cancelled because of poor Lord Raydon, and I had such a lovely part.'

'I expect it'll be revived later on,' Averil told her indifferently.

'I don't know, they do say Her Ladyship is thinking of giving it up. Shouldn't be surprised if she got married again, she's still a beautiful woman.'

'Have you any idea who?' Averil asked with a faint hope that some unknown man would be mentioned.

'I haven't heard anyone actually named. It wouldn't be right with His Lordship only just gone, but he was away so much she must have been lonesome. I did think she had a soft spot for that director chap who helped us out with *Quality Street*. Shouldn't be surprised at all if it turned out he was an old flame. She might even go back to the stage. I mean ... how old would she be, about forty? That's no age nowadays, and he was a good-looker. They'd make a lovely pair, wouldn't you say?'

'They would,' Averil agreed, turning the knife in her wound, and changed the subject.

On Monday Averil hired a car to take her to Colchester and went back to London. She could afford such extravagances, for she did not spend much of her salary beyond her modest keep at Mrs. Reubens', and now she was on full pay. She decided that she would invest in some new clothes, and ask Cecily, who was much more fashion-conscious than she was, to help her choose them. John had had a point there, she did not make the most of herself. When she arrived at the theatre, involuntarily she looked round for Philip, but of course he was not there, nor was there any message from him among the mail fixed to the board. She had not expected any, but there was always hope.

Cecily was enthusiastic about the shopping expedition.

'You must do something about your hair,' she told her. 'It's time you had those rat's tails cut off. Since you wear a wig and presumably often will in future productions, it would be easier if it were short.'

About to protest, for there would be no future production, Averil changed her mind. She had preserved her adolescent image too long and it was time she looked more sophisticated. She had her hair cut and curled, showing the shape of her head. She bought a smart trouser suit and a classical one in plain colours with scarves and handkerchief squares in brilliant prints to wear with them, silk and lace blouses and, most extravagant of all, a mink stole.

'Later you ought to have a mink coat,' Cecily remarked, 'but since they're a bit pricey you'd better wait until you've got a husband to give you one.'

'An unlikely contingency,' Averil told her.

'Of course you'll marry, actresses always do, usually several times. Surely you aren't moping for John?'

Because of Averil's reticence where Philip was concerned, it had not occurred to Cecily that it could be anyone else. She had noted that he appeared to have a yen for her sister, but that seemed to have faded.

Averil assured her that she had no regrets for John, then asked with assumed carelessness if she knew where Philip Conway was.

'Ian says he was so worn out by his efforts to make

us presentable in *Romeo* his doctor has sent him away on a cruise,' Cecily informed her, adding flippantly, 'Knowing our Philip I bet he didn't go alone.'

'No, I don't suppose he did,' Averil agreed flatly.

So that was where Lady Raydon had gone.

Three days later Averil found Philip in her dressing room when she came off after her final curtain. He was sitting upon her dressing stool exchanging quips with Maudie, wearing a white polo-necked sweater under a dark jacket, and far from looking bronzed by a sea trip, he was pale, with dark smudges under his eyes. She halted in the doorway, utterly amazed at the sight of him. The thin white negligée she wore for her last appearance swathed her limbs and the heavy tresses of her black wig covered her like a cloak. Her eyes were dark pools still reflecting the anguish she had been simulating, but as she beheld her visitor, they began to glow.

'Philip,' she murmured.

He rose to his feet and snapped his fingers at the dresser.

'My good woman—out!'

'I'm not your good woman,' Maudie returned sturdily. 'It's my job to get Miss Avon changed and by rights you shouldn't be here. Telling me to get out indeed!'

Philip heaved a mock sigh.

'She dares to flout my authority. Alas for democracy! I can no longer have you whipped for insubordination.'

'The very idea! I've my duty to do, sir.'

'Far be it from me to prevent you, but I need to have a few words with Miss Avon in private.' He produced his notecase. 'Perhaps that will soothe your ruffled feelings,' he held out a note. 'Now go and get lost for the next ten minutes.'

Maudie took the money. 'Seeing as you was in authority here . . .' she began.

'And still am,' he cut her short. 'And don't you stand listening outside the door.'

'Oh, sir, as if I would!' she told him reproachfully, as she went out.

'Just what she meant to do, nosey baggage,' Philip said, striding to the door and closing it after a precautionary glance down the passage. 'You have a conscientious chaperone, my love.'

He stood with his back to the door gazing down at Averil, as she subsided on to her stool. 'Well, how did it go tonight?'

'The same as usual,' she said listlessly, wondering what he had come to say. So like him to waste time bandying words with Maudie while she was on tenderhooks, but he had probably only looked in to see how the play was progressing.

'It's running more smoothly than it did at the start. I was in front, you know.'

'Then why did you ask?'

'I wanted your opinion, but I see you aren't much interested.' Voice and manner changed. 'You weren't a flop, Averil.'

His eyes, very blue and intent, were fixed upon her significantly, but Averil did not look at him. She lifted off her heavy wig and heard his startled exclamation.

'My God, what have you done to yourself?'

She ran a comb through her flattened hair and it sprayed out like a fine brown web about her face.

'I've had my hair cut.'

'How dare you, without consulting me!'

'Did I have to do that?' She turned her head to face him. 'I've been told you hadn't been too well and I hope you're recovered.'

'I did have a throat affection, but it's cleared up

152

now, else I'd have been round before.' She noticed his voice was slightly husky.

'I'm sorry. I heard you'd gone on a cruise.'

'I could do with one, a bit of sunshine would be very welcome after all the gloomy weather we've been having, but I wouldn't go away without seeing you, Averil, surely you didn't think that?'

She turned back to her mirror. 'I ... I don't know what to think.'

He came to stand behind her and she could see his face mirrored in the glass in front of her.

'Surely you knew I was expecting your answer?' he said reproachfully. 'You've been back to Elmsford, haven't you? I hope you gave young Woods his congé.'

'We've parted,' she said briefly.

'That's something, but what's the matter, Averil? Are you annoyed because I didn't come to you at once? I'd lost my voice, and not being the Frog Prince, I objected to croaking in your presence.'

He spoke lightly, but he was studying her irresponsive face closely in the mirror. 'Averil!' He spoke her name insistently.

'You hadn't developed your bad throat on the first night,' she said quietly, 'but you didn't come near me. You were with Lady Raydon.'

'I meant to come, but I had to take her back to her hotel—after all, she's just lost her husband, and *Romeo and Juliet* is not the cheeriest spectacle for someone who has been bereaved. She was rather ... overcome. Besides, I thought you'd be celebrating with your family, and by next day my temperature was soaring.'

'If Lady Raydon was overcome I don't think it was with grief for the loss of her husband,' Averil observed with unwonted acidity. 'And I fancy you and she had a little celebrating to do, now she's free. You were engaged to her once, weren't you?'

She marvelled at her own calmness, but Philip's words had recalled all the hurt of the past few days. She did not doubt that he had been ill, but he could have sent a message to reassure her.

'What if I was?' he asked coldly. 'It came to nothing, and it's you I've asked to marry me.'

She fidgeted with the make-up sticks on the table before her.

'I won't hold you to that,' she told him, looking down at her restless fingers so that all he could see of her eyes were the long silky lashes veiling them. 'When you proposed to me you didn't know Lord Raydon was going to be killed. I've always guessed there was someone in your life for whom you'd cared very deeply and I wouldn't want to ... to ...' her voice trembled, but she went on resolutely, '... stand in your way now you can gain your heart's desire.'

'What drivel are you talking now? Sounds like a novelette!' His hands clamped down on her shoulders, feeling the slight bones beneath his fingers. 'You know what I want most—to make you a great actress. As for what was between me and Gina, that was a long time ago. It's the future—your future—I'm interested in, not the past.'

She twisted out of his hold, and springing to her feet turned to face him; the effort of freeing herself had torn the drapery from her creamy shoulders, their natural colour merging with the make-up that still covered her face and neck. The shading round her eyes made them look enormous and they glittered with the tears she was too proud to shed. She could have posed for the Tragic Muse herself.

'I don't want to be a great actress,' she cried despairingly. 'All I want is ...' She was going to say 'your love', but checked herself. Philip had no love to give her, perhaps Georgina had killed his capacity for love. 'I don't believe you've got a heart,' she went on feverishly, 'or if you have it's atrophied. All you care about is power, power to make your puppets do your bidding. I won't marry you, Philip, and become your marionette...'

'Oh, yes, you will,' he interrupted. 'You can't help yourself. You became mine when you accepted the part in my production, and just to demonstrate how helpless you are...' His arms went round her, drawing her against himself. Through the thin material of her dress she could feel through the rough wool of his sweater the rapid beat of his heart. 'My leading lady,' he murmured, 'the brightest star in the theatrical firmament.' His grip tightened, and his mouth came down upon hers, bruising, possessive, punishing. Averil was lost. She had so hungered for him and now he was holding her as if he meant never to let her go. His grip was cruelly close, but she felt no pain, only wild ecstasy, melting in his embrace, submerged in the clamour of her senses. Let him do what he would with her, so long as he kept her beside him.

A tentative tap on the door, which had opened a crack, heralded the presence of Maudie. Philip released Averil with a muttered oath as the woman sidled into the room.

'Beg pardon, sir, but it's getting very late,' she said, smirking. 'I'll be missing my last bus, and you wouldn't want to have to run me home, would you, with so much else on your mind?'

'Oh dear, I hope none of my poor fans are still waiting for me,' Averil exclaimed, for she had become used to the nightly siege, and however late she was, there were usually a few stalwarts hoping for her autograph.

'I'll deal with those,' Philip announced. 'Tell 'em you've given them the slip. But how do you get home?

Where's that sister of yours?'

'She makes her own arrangements, and I've a car laid on every night. It'll be waiting too.'

She reached for a tissue and began to remove the make-up from her face. Philip glanced at his ruefully in the mirror to find it plentifully bedaubed with grease and powder. He hastily and efficiently wiped it away.

'I'll find your car and be waiting outside for you,' he told her. 'Of course I'll see you safely home.'

'Really, I'll be quite all right—and should you be out so late if you haven't been well?'

'Don't fuss,' he said irritably. 'I'm fully recovered, and now everything's settled it's my privilege to take charge of you.'

He went out and Averil hastened to put on her street clothes. Though she had not given him an affirmation in words, he took it for granted that she had surrendered to his will. But there were no more caresses that night; during the short drive to Blooms-bury he talked of nothing except his future plans for her, and did not even give her a goodnight kiss.

They did not announce their engagement at once, though Philip was planning to be married when the run of the Shakespeare play was ended. That would be at Christmas when the Regina was needed for panto-mime; it had been rented upon only a three months' lease. As the play was filling the theatre to capacity the management had the option of finding it another home or sending out a Number One Tour. It chose the latter, but Gemma was to play Juliet, Philip insisting that Averil must remain in town. He was absorbed in plans for the modern play in which he wanted her to play the lead, and after their marriage they were to live in his flat, for she would have little time for house-keeping.

'Some day I'd like a house by the river, like Mrs. Brent's,' Averil told him wistfully.

'Some day we'll have one,' he promised, 'but for the present it'll be much more convenient to be nearer to theatreland.'

Naturally it could not be kept from Cecily, though she was sworn to silence.

'I always thought he was sweet on you,' that lady announced. 'But I didn't think he was the marrying kind. He's a vast improvement on John and he'll be able to advance your career.'

Averil winced. If only Philip was marrying her for love and she could spend her time looking after his home and, God willing, bearing his children. To her shy hints about a family he returned:

'Later, Averil, we may consider it, but you've a long way to go first. When you're fully established maybe, but it would be fatal to your prospects to drop out now.'

So the dream of a riverside home and children like Ivor and Tess had to be relegated to an uncertain future.

But nothing could entirely dim Averil's joy and satisfaction in the fact that she was about to become Philip's wife. However divergent their viewpoints, and for whatever reasons he wanted her, he was prepared to forge that strongest of bonds between them. Physically she knew they were compatible, though Philip was sparing with his demonstrations, but she had seen the blue flame in his eyes when he looked at her, and knew with feminine intuition that he desired her body as well as her success. She only prayed it would not be transitory.

One morning, when she had come down to breakfast, Mrs. Reubens told her that a woman had rung up to enquire if she were available.

'I didn't want to disturb you, you need your rest,' Rachel said, 'so I took the liberty of saying you'd be in this morning. She'll be round about eleven.'

'Did she give her name?'

'No, and I forgot to ask for it. Nice spoken she was, probably a reporter.'

'I suppose I must see her,' Averil sighed. She had endured several interviews, good publicity, Philip had told her, but she did not enjoy them.

At eleven o'clock the daily help called her, saying that she had shown the visitor into Mrs. Reubens' private sanctum so that they would not be disturbed.

The gas fire was full on, making the ornate room with its heavy furnishings seem a little stuffy. The photographs of the dear departeds peered down curiously at the stylish woman seated in the velvet-covered chair by the window. Averil came to a halt, overcome by surprise. It was Lady Raydon.

CHAPTER NINE

MEASURED by actual days and weeks it was not long since Averil and Georgina Mortimer, Lady Raydon, had last met, but so much had happened in that short space of time that it seemed much longer. She had changed from the naïve young girl that Lady Raydon had befriended into someone much more mature. She was not nearly so innocent now, Philip and life at the theatre had educated her and it had been revealed that Lady Raydon was far from being the paragon that she had thought her.

Yet when Averil beheld her again, she reverted momentarily to the youngster she had been in a surge of nostalgic memories, which eliminated the incomprehensible estrangement that seemed to have occurred, recollecting only the many happy hours that she had spent under Georgina's tutelage. She went towards her visitor with a radiant face and outstretched hands, which Lady Raydon, rising from her chair, took in both of hers. She seemed equally pleased to see Averil and kissed her warmly.

'Averil, my dear child!' she exclaimed. 'It seems ages since we met and I haven't yet congratulated you upon your success. All the Thespians are so proud of you, including myself.'

Georgina was wearing a black well cut classical suit, which suited her svelte figure and pink and white complexion, with a white blouse and a black and white turban-shaped hat on her impeccably waved fair hair. She looked very much the great lady.

'I'm ever so pleased to see you, Lady Raydon, and so glad you've looked me up,' Averil said sincerely. 'Would you like some coffee? Mrs. Reubens usually has some percolating about now.'

'No, thank you, I can't stop long,' Georgina told her, resuming her seat. 'You've heard of my loss?' Averil nodded sympathetically. 'Poor Arthur, I was always afraid something would happen to him in those outlandish places. Naturally I'm very much upset and my doctor advises me to go away, and a cruise in the Bahamas has been suggested. A very good idea, don't you think, now autumn is almost upon us.'

'I'm sure it is,' Averil agreed as she sat down opposite to her visitor. The mention of a cruise was ominous since she had heard it mentioned in connection with Philip, and though he had reproached her for thinking he would go away without seeing her, he had not denied the possibility.

Lady Raydon went on with a fine show of cordiality that did not quite ring true:

'I'm trying to persuade Philip Conway to come with me. You know we're old friends and he's been ill. He doesn't seem to me to be picking up as he should do. He put me off with a lot of blah about a new play in which it appears you're expecting to star. I came to ask if it couldn't be postponed until he's better. In fact I'm hoping you'll add your persuasions to mine, as it's your interests he's considering. Would you mind desperately if the new play were postponed?'

'I wouldn't mind if it never came off at all,' Averil said candidly, 'but my persuasions carry very little weight with Mr. Conway.'

'Oh, really?' Georgina looked a little nonplussed. 'I gather that he's afraid that if it is put off, you might be tempted to accept other engagements when *Romeo and Juliet* finishes. You must be very flattered, my dear, that he thinks such a lot of your work.'

She was studying the girl opposite to her, noting her short, wavy hair that curled bewitchingly about her mobile face, the smart simplicity of her trouser suit. Averil had improved, and Philip was nearing the age when mature men were apt to be attracted by youth, but she did not believe Averil could possibly constitute a serious rival.

'I'd never dream of doing any such thing,' Averil declared vehemently, 'and if Mr. Conway wants to go on this cruise, he'll go without consulting me, but perhaps he doesn't want to go.'

'Indeed?' Lady Raydon looked a little taken aback by this forthrightness. Then leaning forward, she said confidentially:

'I'm very fond of Philip, and I've his welfare very much at heart. Unfortunately, long ago, we had a slight misunderstanding. He chose to take umbrage at a foolish action of mine, but he's been perfectly sweet to me since my widowhood, so all is forgiven. If only we could rid him of his obsession with this play, I'm sure he'd be willing to come with me, and the sea air would do him the world of good. He really does need a rest.'

Averil knew that Lady Raydon was exaggerating Philip's ill health to disguise her real motives; he had recovered completely from his indisposition. She said firmly:

'I'm afraid I can't help you, Lady Raydon, but I doubt very much if Philip would go anywhere with you. You see, he has ... other commitments besides the play.'

A lovely colour rose in her cheeks, and her big eyes became luminous, betraying her utterly to the woman facing her.

Georgina's friendliness vanished and her grey eyes became hostile.

'My dear child!' she exclaimed. 'Didn't I warn you? Surely you haven't been so foolish as to become emotionally involved with him?'

'I'm afraid I have,' Averil told her with devastating honesty. 'Actually, we're about to announce our engagement.'

'You and Philip? No, no, it's utterly unsuitable!'

Averil said, her eyes sparkling with mischief:

'I believe he's considered to be quite a good match.'

Lady Raydon seemed to shrink, suddenly she looked quite old, and her expression was venomous.

'You must have misunderstood him,' she snapped.

'I don't think so, Lady Raydon. He was very explicit.'

Lady Raydon rose abruptly and walked to the window and stood with her back to Averil looking out at the square bathed in September sunshine. The girl eyed her taut figure wistfully. She might have known Georgina had not come to renew their old friendship, it was Philip who had come between them. Presently Lady Raydon turned round, all enmity wiped from her face, which expressed only compassion.

'My poor little girl,' she began, and her voice was honey-sweet. 'He doesn't mean it, he couldn't be serious about a chit like you. No doubt you've got a crush on him, that's only natural, and he's misled you. Men of his age are often drawn to very young girls, but Philip's got more sense than to marry one. It's possible he may have been revenging himself upon me by paying you attention. He can be a little vindictive, but as for marriage—no, he's only using you as a stooge. What's become of that nice young man you were so fond of?'

'I didn't love John,' Averil told her composedly. 'And I'm growing up. I'd hate to think Philip is as mean as you're trying to make out. Nor is he exactly Methuselah, he's younger than you are, I believe.' She could not resist that thrust. She had learned that Philip was thirty-six and Georgina was over forty. 'And I don't see what business it is of yours.'

A bright spot of colour showed on Lady Raydon's cheeks, as she made an obvious effort to control herself.

'It is my business because I'm the only woman he's ever loved. Until recently I wasn't free, but now I am.' She looked at Averil significantly. 'We were once engaged, you see.'

'He told me that,' Averil returned, 'and I also know that you threw him over to marry Lord Raydon and that has embittered him. He believes all women are perfidious and mercenary.'

'Including yourself?'

Averil smiled wryly. 'He hopes that as I'm so young he's caught me before I've had time to be corrupted.'

'Oh, stuff!' Lady Raydon exclaimed rudely. She fretted with the strap of her handbag. Then she said in a changed voice, with almost a note of pleading:

'Don't judge me too hardly. Philip was only a struggling actor when I first knew him and I'd had too much poverty to endure. Lord Raydon offered me security and there was none with Philip, we didn't know his father would leave him anything, we thought he'd been disinherited. But the fact that Philip took it so hard shows how much he loved me. It was a long time before I could persuade him to visit me, but when he came, I knew he loved me still, there are unmistakable signs ... And Arthur was so much away. I hoped he'd assuage my loneliness.'

'But, Lady Raydon, you were married!' Averil exclaimed, shocked.

Lady Raydon smiled. 'It's a permissive age,' she pointed out. 'But there's a puritanical streak in Philip, he didn't fulfil my hopes, though I could see how much he wanted to. Now Arthur's dead and the barrier is gone, and I can offer him so much.'

'Even so, it's me he's asked to marry him,' Averil said drily.

Georgina threw her a barbed glance. 'But didn't he commit himself before he knew Arthur had been killed?' she insinuated.

That was only too true. Philip had proposed during that memorable evening at his flat, and though she had delayed giving him her answer, he might consider he was in honour bound to her, unless she decided to refuse him. Such scruples were rare in this day and age where inclination was given priority but oddly enough Philip had old-fashioned notions. She recalled that on the night of her debut when she had needed him so badly he had not come to her, he had been with Lady Raydon.

As she looked at the woman before her, so beautiful, assured and perfectly groomed, it seemed improbable that Philip could prefer herself, nor could she conceive that the vexed question of her career was of sufficient importance to him to cause him to put it before the consummation of his love for Georgina which had at last become possible. It seemed only too likely that he would find an excuse to repudiate her and capitulate to the older woman.

Seeing the girl's confidence had been shaken, Lady Raydon said persuasively:

'The cruise would be a face-saving expedient all round. If you will release Philip from any promises that he's made you, I'm sure he'll come with me and you'll not lack for work after your success with Juliet. I know you, Averil, you're too proud to want to pick up another woman's leavings. By the time we return, your connection with him will have been forgotten, and in any case you haven't yet made your engagement public. We'll be married quietly when we come back—I don't want any publicity—and by that time you'll have fallen in love with someone else. Young girls are so susceptible.'

'You've got it all taped, haven't you?' Averil observed, 'but there's one factor still to be consulted. I mean Philip himself.'

A flicker of alarm showed in the grey eyes.

'You couldn't be so brash as to go and ask him which of us he prefers?'

'Why not?'

'Well, it would be terribly embarrassing for him to have to tell you point blank that he preferred me. He wouldn't want to hurt you.'

'I don't think that would worry him,' Averil said a little bitterly, 'if he really wanted to be quit of me.'

'You can say that of the man you fancy you love?'

'I know he can be cruel and it's you who've made him so,' Averil accused her. 'But it's much more likely he'll think I'm using you as a pretext to be rid of him. He hasn't much faith in women, and that again is your doing.'

'You're being presumptuous,' Lady Raydon said haughtily.

'I didn't mean to be, but we've reached a point where plain speaking is necessary.'

Lady Raydon sighed. 'You've changed, Averil, you used to be such a retiring, amiable creature. Granted all this is so, and Philip is prepared to marry you, consider this. He needs a decorative wife who can be an asset as a hostess to all the important people he has to entertain. You may not know it, but since his father died, he has wide business interests besides his theatrical enterprises. I would be such a help to him, whereas you're only a gauche country girl with no knowledge of social usages.'

Averil winced, turning away her head, for this was something that she had not considered. She did not know much about Philip's life apart from the theatre, but she did know he had a good many social commitments. On the night when he had asked her to his flat, he had been out and was going out again to some sort of party. That she would have to participate in such functions was an unwelcome thought.

Georgina saw that she had made an impression.

'Men don't think about that sort of thing until it's too late,' she said. 'You'd hate to find yourself inadequate, and you would be.'

'I ... I can't withstand him,' Averil cried, twisting her fingers together. 'If he insists.'

It was Lady Raydon's turn to wince at the implication of this admission.

'Then you must write and tell him it was all a mistake,' she urged. 'Say there's someone else. He can't expect fidelity from an infant like you. Tell him he's too old.' She knew that would wound Philip most.

Averil said slowly: 'I'll think over all you've said, Lady Raydon, but I can't decide anything now,' and with that Georgina had to be content.

Averil showed her out so that Mrs. Reubens never knew that her one-time associate had visited the house. She left Averil considerably shaken. All her life she had paid deference to Lady Raydon and been guided by her advice, and though she was not so naïve as not to know that most of what she had said had been motivated by jealousy, it was not easy to shake off the influence of years, and she was left with a feeling of complete inadequacy for the position she was to fill. But she did not believe Philip would let her go after his arrogant proclamation of ownership, nor did she attach any importance to Lady Raydon's hint that Philip was marrying her to spite his former love. She knew why Philip wanted to marry her. He desired to create a great star and bask in its radiance. Finding her to be pliable and susceptible to his influence, he meant to ensure that she could not run out on him. There was a bizarre Svengali touch about their relationship, and Philip was first and foremost a man of the theatre. He had defied his father and risked his inheritance to go on the stage.

Averil had been shocked to learn that her revered Lady Raydon had been prepared to conduct a liaison with him in her husband's absence. She had always believed her to be immaculate. Philip had repelled her advances out of respect to his absent host when he stayed with her, but he must still have a strong feeling for her if it were upon her account he had remained celibate for so long. Nowadays there was a permissive attitude towards morality and it might well happen that when he discovered Averil's shortcomings, which she feared were many, he would go back to Georgina and consider it no sin. Averil could never countenance that sort of three-cornered situation; it offended all her ideas of romantic love, and that was the crux of the matter—Philip did not recognise love, nor had Averil any desire for the glittering future he persisted in dangling before her. She wanted a husband, home and family, but the last two were remote in this union to which she was committed and she might end up with only half a husband. Philip had assured her that Georgina belonged to his past, but Lady Raydon intended to project herself into his present, and Averil had an uneasy presentiment that eventually she would win him.

Finding the house oppressive, she went out into the streets, intending to go for a long walk, terminating in one of the parks. Being still deeply preoccupied, she was careless of her going. She never reached the park.

It was some time before the sedation cleared sufficiently for Averil to become aware that she was in a hospital ward. Dimly she recalled moments of intense pain, strangers crowding round her and the ambulance's siren. Her first thought was that it must be getting late and she had to give a performance that night. She called feebly.

'So you've come round,' a nurse said, feeling for her pulse. 'Had a bit of a rough time, haven't you, dear, but you'll be better now.'

Averil knit her brows. 'I suppose I've had an accident, but I have to go on tonight.' She tried to raise herself in the bed.

'You lie still, dear. You won't go on tonight, nor for a good many nights to come,' she was told. 'But not to worry, you've got an understudy, haven't you?'

'Yes, of course. How long have I been here?'

'You were brought in the day before yesterday, but you've been under sedation most of the time since then. You were pretty badly knocked about.'

'Does anybody know?' Averil meant Philip.

'Naturally your relations have been advised, but you've talked long enough. Just keep quiet, dear, and later you'll be having some lunch.'

The nurse bustled away and Averil lay back, reflecting that at last Gemma would obtain her chance. As for herself, perhaps her problems were going to be solved in a way she had not anticipated. She was sore and bruised all over and one leg was in plaster. It would be many weeks before she could play Juliet again, and Philip would blame her for being so careless.

He came that afternoon, with a face full of concern and a large bunch of roses. Because of her status and the numerous enquiries about her, Averil was in a side ward where at the moment she was the only occupant.

'Well, you were a little chump,' Philip said kindly. 'Why couldn't you look where you were going? We've all been in a fine state about you.'

'You've got Gemma,' she reminded him.

He made a face. 'Yes, but she's not you. Your parents have been advised and they'll be coming up to see you, also Rosamund, Cecily and a few others when you're allowed to have visitors.'

'But if I'm not allowed to have visitors, how did you get in?'

'They couldn't keep me out,' he told her with a grin. 'But I had to promise to keep very quiet, so you'd better not talk any more.'

He laid a consolatory hand over hers lying on the sheet, reminding her of the time when he had done so upon her first evening in London, and as then, so now, he seemed to transmit something of his strength and vitality to her. He stayed beside her, his lean face quiet and a little withdrawn, until the nurse chivvied him out.

He came every day, and she had many other visitors, including her family, and as she progressed towards recovery, she was able to talk to them all. Her room and the main ward next to it were full of her flowers, for many admirers sent floral tokens.

'It isn't often we have such a celebrity in here,' one of the nurses told her. 'You seem to be popular, dear.'

Her cuts and bruises healed, but her leg was badly fractured. She learned from Cecily that amputation had been threatened, but that Philip had strenuously opposed it.

'He was quite right,' Cecily told her. 'Sister says it's healing satisfactorily and a lot better than they anticipated.'

Averil gazed at her horrorstruck. 'A one-legged Juliet!' she whispered.

'Bernhardt continued to play dramatic parts minus a leg.'

'I'm not a Sarah Barnhardt,' Averil said sharply. 'It's nothing to joke about, Cis. Shall I be ... lame?'

'Of course not. It'll be as good as new when the plaster comes off.'

Rosamund Brent told her that she was arranging for her to be transferred to Riverside House, and her parents were agreeable.

'I've got much more space than they have,' she pointed out. 'And Mrs. White has had nursing experience. You can have a room downstairs with a view of the river. The children will be coming to me for their half-term holiday, and Tess says if you can't walk, you can tell her stories all day, but of course she won't be allowed to worry you.'

'How awfully kind of you,' Averil exclaimed, the tears of weakness springing to her eyes. 'But why should you bother with me?'

'Why shouldn't I? Mrs. White and I have quite a lot of spare time on our hands, and I'd love to have you. Actually it was Philip's idea, he thinks you'll be more accessible there than at Elmsford.' She smiled knowingly. 'Been a bit sly, haven't you, dear? Why didn't you tell me?'

'It . . . it isn't official yet.'

'Isn't it? Everyone seems to know about it, and Philip's been in a frantic stew.'

'He would be. He never did like Gemma's acting.'

'Gemma? Oh, you mean Juliet. She's quite adequate, you know. She gives a very polished performance.'

'Polish being what I lack.'

'Precious stones are polished,' Rosamund said cryptically. 'But they have no feeling. I prefer your interpretation, it had more heart.'

Averil turned her head away. 'I often wish I hadn't so much heart,' she said fretfully. 'It's very inconvenient.'

Mrs. Avon was a little sad that she could not take charge of her daughter, but she had been down to Riverside and had to admit that the accommodation was infinitely superior to what she could provide in her own small house.

'Rosamund says you can come up for the day whenever you like,' Averil tried to comfort her. She herself had no fault to find with the arrangement since it kept her nearer to Philip, and she depended upon his virile strength to sustain her. But before she left the hospital he broke the unwelcome news to her that he had to leave for the States upon an extended visit.

'I hate to have to leave you like this,' he told her, 'but it's rather important. You seem to be progressing very well, and I'd like to get my affairs in order over there before our marriage. There are the rights on a new play I want to bring over here to be discussed, and I'm needed in Los Angeles to disentangle a muddle over some film scripts in which I have an interest. They were made from plays I had sponsored.'

'Will you be away long?' she asked anxiously.

'I'm afraid I may be some weeks, but Rosa will take great care of you.'

'You'll write?'

'I'm not a very brilliant correspondent, and you wouldn't be interested in my business deals, but I'll send you heaps of postcards.'

'That'll be nice,' she said without enthusiasm. What she wanted was a love letter, but Philip no doubt would consider that foolishness. She had been too ill to consider the doubts that had beset her after Lady Raydon's visit, and had been content to let matters slide, and enjoy Philip's daily visits. He could not be indifferent to be so attentive. But now they were beginning to revive. Today Philip seemed a little absent, his mind engaged with his affairs. He must be finding the continual hospital visits tedious and be glad of an excuse to discontinue them. Because of a growing misgiving, she asked anxiously:

'You will come back, Philip?'

'But of course.' He looked astonished. 'What made you ask that?'

'I don't know how soon I'll be well,' she faltered. 'Sometimes I feel I'll never walk again.'

'Rubbish, child, don't harbour such morbid thoughts,' he bade her. 'Broken limbs heal with patience and you'll be okay for my next play.'

Averil shrank back into her pillows. Was that the reason for his constant attention? He was checking upon her progress, planning for his next production, and she had dared to hope he was motivated by a personal regard for her. Once in America, he would dismiss her from his thoughts, absorb himself in the business of the hour, and expect her to be recovered and waiting for him on his return, to be pushed into his next play after a brief interlude for marriage, which only meant to him a means to an end.

As it was the normal visiting period, Cecily and Ian came in to create a diversion from her sombre thoughts. Their arms were full of offerings, fruit, flowers and magazines.

'I hear you're off on a sea trip,' MacAllister said to Philip.

Philip shrugged his shoulders. 'By the time I could book a reservation on a plane, I found I'd get there faster by boat.'

'The voyage will do you good,' Ian observed. 'You're looking peaky, old man. Mind you relax for a few days.'

'I've had an anxious time,' Philip returned with his eyes on Averil, 'but now I can relax with an easy mind.'

'And in pleasant company,' Cecily said with assumed innocence.

'I don't care for shipboard acquaintances,' Philip announced, casually. He stooped over Averil. 'Goodbye, little one. I hope when I come back you'll be on your feet again and come running to meet me.'

He touched her cheek lightly with his fingertips, but he did not kiss her. He rarely did if others were present.

Averil watched his lean lithe figure disappear down

the ward, with a feeling of constriction about her heart. When and how would she see him again? The mention of a voyage had brought Lady Raydon back into her mind. Philip did not look back and when the swing doors had closed behind him, she turned to Cecily, asking suspiciously:

'Why did you mention pleasant company? Lady Raydon isn't by any chance crossing to the States?'

'What on earth put that idea into your head?' Cecily returned, but she did not look at her. 'I haven't a clue as to where Her Ladyship is.'

Averil had had no time to tell her sister about Georgina's visit to her before the accident, yet she suspected that Cecily knew something and had been unable to resist a dig at Philip. It was significant that Philip was not flying to America, and his excuse about a reservation seemed a little thin. Depressed by his departure, weakened by her condition, Averil was a prey to nervous fears and exaggerated suspicions. If Lady Raydon was also travelling upon Philip's ship, she was sure she would be able to persuade him to her way of thinking, and she would never see him again.

Averil's spirits revived a little when she arrived at Riverside House. Although it was late in October the surrounding country was still bright with autumn tints, the beech trees in the neighbourhood being a glorious russet brown, the willows and aspens pale gold. Mrs. White was an efficient nurse and seemed delighted to take charge of the patient and revive her old skill. Averil rose every morning, dressed and lay on a chaise-longue in front of the window, watching the slow-moving river and the craft that used it from launches to rowing boats and sailing dinghies. At half term the children arrived, and Tess was always in her room. She begged Mrs. Brent to let her stay, declaring that she enjoyed her company. The little girl played with her model theatre and together they invented marvellous plays to be enacted by the chessmen. The knights were Tess's favourite pieces, performing immaginary feats of incredible valour. Ivor would bring in trophies from the garden to show her—a spray of scarlet hips, an intriguingly shaped pebble, or one of Lohengrin's feathers.

From Philip came postcards, of New York, Florida, where he had tracked down an author he wished to contact, and later San Francisco and Los Angeles. When he gave her an address, she wrote in reply, but they were stilted little letters, for she dared not express what was in her heart. Thus the weeks slipped by and she grew steadily stronger.

Philip was still away when Mrs. White took Averil up to London to have the plaster removed from her leg. The bones had knitted, but it seemed pitifully weak and inadequate to support her. Various treatments were prescribed, and noticing her disconsolate expression, the doctor told her frankly: 'You don't realise, Miss Avon, how fortunate you are to have your leg still; it was broken in several places and the muscles were injured. In time you'll be able to walk, though you'll always have a slight limp, and may need a walking stick for support.'

Juliet with a limp, Philip's new heroine using a walking stick! Averil knew her career was finished.

'He shouldn't have told you that,' Mrs. Brent exclaimed, when a stony-faced Averil gave her the doctor's verdict upon her return from the theatre that night.

'I wanted to know the truth,' Averil told her. 'He thinks I'm very fortunate.'

'He was being pessimistic,' Rosamund declared. 'Didn't want to raise your hopes, but it will get all right in time, I'm sure. You're young, and with proper treatment you'll walk as well as you ever did.'

'But it'll take ages and ages, and I'll soon be forgotten. No, Rosamund, I've decided I'll give up the stage.'

'Well, you haven't lost everything,' Mrs. Brent said consolingly. 'And I've often thought it was better when the wife wasn't working professionally. You've still got Philip, and your injury won't prohibit being a good wife and mother.'

'I'm afraid Philip was only interested in the actress,' Averil told her with a quivering lip. 'I shall of course write and release him at once. He'll have no use for me now.'

'My dear, you're wronging him.' Mrs. Brent looked shocked. 'He'll have the greatest sympathy for your wrecked career, and . . .'

'I don't want his pity, if he's got any,' Averil interrupted stormily. 'I want his love, and that I've never had. At this moment I've reason to suppose he's amusing himself with an old flame in America.'

And she flung herself into Mrs. Brent's arms in a passion of tears.

Rosamund soothed and calmed her as a mother might. She must not distress herself over a mere supposition, she would retard her recovery. Now she must go to bed and she would bring her a hot drink. In the morning, after a good sleep, she would take a more rational view of the situation.

Averil did sleep long and soundly, for her hostess had given her a sleeping pill. She awoke in a mood of calm resignation. She would return home at once, she decided, she had imposed upon Mrs. Brent's kindness long enough, and it was not as if she were completely immobile. As soon as possible she would ask for her job back with the solicitors; a limp or even a crutch would not hinder her typing. But before she did anything else she must write to Philip, and that would not be easy because she had no wish to appeal to the compassion that Mrs Brent had mentioned. She must give no hint of her heartbreak, nor show regret at the loss of her profession. The latter would not be difficult, for she only had to reiterate that she had never wanted to be a famous actress. Regarding their engagement, she told him that she had come to realise that a union between them would be most unsuitable. Setting her lips, she stoically mentioned the gap in age, which had never troubled her, but about which she had been told he was sensitive. She concluded by saying she was sure she would be happier back in her old environment and that coming to London had been a big mistake. She signed herself:

'Your little country mouse.'

She permitted herself one catty touch, adding a postscript to the effect that she hoped he and Lady Raydon were enjoying their reunion in America.

That'll show him I'm not quite the gullible little idiot he believes me to be, she thought as she wrote the address, and then her heart twisted with a spasm of pain as she realised they were severed for all time.

Her letter written, she asked Mrs. White to post it for her and proceeded to make her plans for going home. It was the beginning of the week and she thought she would be ready to go by the end of it, when she was more used to the crutch which had been given to her to take the weight off her injured leg. She could hire a car to take her to Elmsford. At that point Mrs. Avon rang up from a callbox to enquire how she had fared with the doctor, and Averil was able to tell her her plans.

'It's all right, Mummy, don't be upset,' she said in answer to her mother's dismayed ejaculation. 'I'm not bothered, I never did care for London and I'm just longing to be home again.'

'But Mr. Conway ... I mean ... weren't you ...'

'Oh, that's all washed up. He's gone to America. Didn't I tell you?'

She was in a fever to be away and to cut off all connection with her London life. Soon, she thought drearily, it would come to seem like a glittering dream without reality, but the ache in her heart when she thought of Philip was too painfully real. Ergo, she must stop her thoughts from straying towards him and in time he too would become part of the dream.

Mrs. Brent was reluctant to let her go, but conceded that her parents must be anxious to have her home again. Averil did not mention Philip.

Two mornings later she was surprised to receive a letter from John. She stared unbelievingly at his familar hand on the envelope, wondering what on earth had inspired him to communicate with her. It transpired he had met her father, who had given him the latest news of her, including her imminent return home.

'I can't tell you how sorry I am to hear about your accident,' he wrote. 'I've been wondering if I dared to write to you and as you're coming home I've decided to do so. You must be greatly distressed by the collapse of all your hopes, and we'll have to try to find consolation for you at Elmsford. Although Lady Raydon had retired, the Thespians are still going strong and I'm sure their new and energetic producer will be delighted to welcome you. You were quite wrong about Clarice, she was all right for a bit of fun, but she's not the sort of girl I'd want to marry. I've always thought a lot of you, and now you're coming back, perhaps you'll give me another chance.' In a postcript he added: 'I've had a wonderful bit of luck with the pools, so I've paid off Conway and got something in hand towards a house.'

Averil felt a surge of revived affection for her former suitor. She was not one to bear malice and she understood now what had needled him. He needed to be the dominant partner and her rise to fame had totally eclipsed his own modest success; he had no wish to be known as Mr. Averil Avon! She was gratified that he still wanted to marry her. He was much more what she required in a husband than Philip, if only her heart had not strayed, but it had, and when she returned home she would be leaving what she most loved behind her.

Rosamund persuaded her to stay over the weekend so that she could say goodbye to the children. Mrs. Brent fetched them on the Sunday afternoon from school when they were allowed to be taken out by any relatives who wished to do so.

'I shan't have anyone to play theatres with me,' Tess said mournfully when the news was broken to her. 'You were super at it.'

'I don't live here,' Averil told her gently. 'I've got my own home to go to and a mummy and daddy who want me.'

'They must be awfully old,' Ivor commented, surveying her.

'As old as Granny?' Tess asked.

'Not quite,' Averil laughed, realising that to the children all adults appeared old.

'I've something to tell you, dears,' said Mrs Brent. 'Your mummy and daddy are coming home shortly. Their film is finished and they'll be staying here.'

Averil flashed her a grateful look, guessing she had not mentioned her daughter's return before in case her visitor felt she must go to make room for them.

'So you won't miss me,' she said to Tess.

' 'Course I shall,' the child told her indignantly, 'but it'll be lovely to have Mummy and Daddy home again.'

Mrs. Brent had to take the children back to school after tea, and when she had gone Averil, feeling tired, lay down on the couch in the sitting room.

'I'll make you a nice cup of tea,' Mrs. White told her, putting a rug over her feet. 'Them youngsters are a bit rumbustious for an invalid.'

How kind everyone is, Averil thought, as she lay back with closed eyes. It's almost worth having an accident to find that out. Her colleagues at the theatre had all sent messages and flowers, including Gemma and Nigel, though their attentions might be a sop to their consciences for their relief at her departure. Still, they had made a gesture.

A car stopped outside the house, and Averil hoped it was not a visitor, as Rosamund could not be back for some time, but Mrs. White would not let anybody in. She heard the chime of the front door bell, the house-keeper's shuffling footsteps, and the murmur of voices. Then to her surprised dismay, the sitting room door opened. She stared blankly at the person who came in while every vestige of colour vanished from her face. Forgetting her disability, she tried to struggle to her feet, while she gasped his name.

'Philip!'

She did indeed try to run to meet him, but her leg gave way, and she collapsed ignominiously at his feet.

CHAPTER TEN

'IDIOT, stupid unmitigated little idiot!' Philip said, as he lifted her up and laid her back on the couch. He ran a light hand over her bandaged leg. 'Haven't hurt it, have you?' he asked anxiously.

She shook her head dumbly, and he went on:

'You look as white as a ghost. Where does Rosa keep her brandy?'

At last Averil found her voice. 'I ... I don't want any, Philip, and I thought you were a ghost.'

He bent over her and kissed her lips with a close hard pressure, and the colour flooded back into her cheeks.

'That seemed to have been as efficacious as brandy,' he said with satisfaction, 'besides convincing you I'm no phantom.'

'But ... but what are you doing here? You were in Los Angeles...'

'I left as soon as I got your damn silly letter. I've been travelling ever since.' He sank wearily into an armchair. 'What sort of a heel do you think I am, Averil?' The lean brown face, bronzed by alien sunshine, was full of reproach.

'I never thought you were a heel,' she told him, 'but don't you understand? I shan't be able to act any more.'

'That remains to be seen,' he said shortly.

'Well, not for a very, very long time even if a miracle occurs, so naturally I supposed...'

Mrs. White came in with the tea tray.

'Your cuppa, miss. Will you have one too, sir?'

'Actually I could do with something a bit stronger. I know Mrs. Brent won't mind.'

'That she won't. She'd never grudge you anything, sir. I'll get the decanter and a glass.'

'Thanks, Mrs. White, you're a ministering angel.'

'Go on, sir. Fine sort of angel I'd make with my flat feet!' She went to the sideboard and took out a cut glass decanter half full of whisky and a tumbler. 'Do you want any soda? There's a syphon in the pantry.'

'No, thanks, I'll take it neat.'

He poured himself a couple of fingers, while Mrs. White attended to Averil's tea.

'Won't you stay and have a cup with me?' Averil asked, suddenly reluctant to be alone with Philip.

Catching his steely eye, Mrs. White refused. 'I know what they say,' she said slyly. 'Two's company and three's none.'

'Excellent sentiment,' Philip told her, smiling.

The door closed upon her exit and he looked at Averil who was busying herself with her tea cup.

'Did you feel you needed a chaperon?' he enquired with a dangerous glitter in his eyes. 'I'm not intending to assault you, though that would be no more than you deserve.'

'What have I done?' she asked, bewildered.

'Oh, nothing, merely supposed that because you've been hurt, I'll repudiate you. You wounded me very deeply, Averil.'

'But, Philip,' she raised herself on her arms the better to observe him, 'there's no reason why you should stick to me. I can't be your leading lady any longer, you'll have to find someone else to play that part you're so keen on, and since I know ...' She stopped, staring at him in sudden doubt. She had been going to say she was only valuable to him as an actress, but could she be wrong? He had come hotfoot from the States to answer her letter in person.

'May be you will play it some day,' he returned, and her raised hopes sank. He was banking upon a miraculous recovery, but that was unlikely. Even Philip's iron will could not put strength into weakened bones and torn muscles.

'Were you really intending to go back to Elmsford without seeing me again?' he asked.

'It seemed the easiest way,' she explained. 'I mean to take up my old life. I was so afraid that if I saw you again, you would pity me . . .'

'What's wrong with pity? It's a very human emotion and it's supposed to be akin to love.'

'But it isn't love,' she said steadily. 'Oh, don't let's beat about the bush, Philip. Perhaps you do feel you ought to stand by me, but I freely absolve you from any obligation. I . . . I'll be happier in Elmsford.' She turned her head away, and her fingers picked at the rug which Mrs. White had replaced over her legs. 'A cripple can't have any place in your life.'

'What utter nonsense! You won't be a cripple.'

'The doctor says I may always have a limp. A halting Juliet, can you imagine it?' She broke into hysterical laughter.

'Stop it!' He sprang up from his chair and struck her quite sharply across the face. 'Drink your tea.' He reached for the cup which she had put down on the window ledge behind her. He waited while she regained control of herself, and obediently sipped the drink. 'Now you listen to me,' he went on, looming over her. 'It doesn't make a ha'porth of difference to me whether you've one leg or two, whether you walk with a limp or crawl on all fours. You're my girl, and it's my privilege to look after you. Go back to your old life, indeed! You'll tell me next you've taken up with Woods again.'

Averil put down her cup and a faint sparkle came into her eyes.

'Well, he did write . . .'

'The devil he did!' He hooked a light high-backed chair towards him with his foot, and sat down beside her and looked at her with an oddly rueful expression.

'I thought you set such store upon true love, but when it's offered to you, you don't recognise it.'

She stared wide-eyed and disbelievingly into his face.

'You don't mean . . . you can't love me.'

'Why not? Am I so monstrous you think I'm incapable of finer feelings?'

'I know you loved Lady Raydon . . .' she began hesitantly.

'Gina? That was over years ago, and a proper sap I was over her, but I was very young. For years I've let her loss embitter me, without realising I'd had a lucky escape.'

'But you stayed with her at the Towers.'

'Occasionally, and never when she was alone, except that last time, and then the boys were home. It gave me great satisfaction to discover that my old obsession with her was completely dead and I was seeing her at last as she really was—a vain selfish creature, who couldn't even be true to the man she'd married for his fortune. Why do you suppose Arthur spent all his time on zoo quests? He was an easygoing fellow, but he wasn't so thick-skinned that he didn't realise she'd nothing but contempt for him once she'd got her hands on his cheque book. But I wasn't going to cuckold him to satisfy her vanity, as I told her repeatedly. She couldn't believe that I'd ceased to desire her.'

'So she didn't go to America with you?'

'Good God, no! Whatever made you think that?'

'Because she told me she was trying to persuade you to go away with her, that now she was free you would marry her.'

'Whenever was this?'

'She came to see me on the day I had my accident. She pointed out what an unsuitable wife I was for you. I think that's why I walked under that bus or whatever it was, I was so upset.'

'The interfering bitch! I suppose she thought that as she could cut no ice with me, she'd try you. But, my darling, why couldn't you trust me?'

He reached for her hand and holding it between his own, stroked it gently, while his anxious eyes searched her face.

'Because I thought my only hold over you was your interest in my acting and Averil Avon was only somebody whose talent you wanted to exploit.'

'So I did,' he returned to her chagrin, 'you see, I thought it was my only hold over you.'

'You knew that wasn't true, didn't I tell you . . .'

'You loved me? Darling, that pathetic little confession couldn't be relied upon, you'd experienced the first stirrings of your womanhood, but I feared it was only an infantile crush you felt towards me, but I was base enough to take advantage of it to the extent of trying to tie you to me. I could at least protect and guide you, and when you'd got over it, you would at least have some gratitude towards me for having made you famous. It would be some compensation for allowing me to trap you.'

'Oh, Philip, how could you be so absurd?' She turned her hand in his and pinched his wrist viciously. 'I didn't care in the least about being famous, and you nearly broke my heart. I thought you . . . didn't care.'

She looked at him with all her heart in her eyes, but to her dismay he did not respond. He withdrew his hands and stared into her face a little bleakly.

'Averil, I've done you a great wrong. When I met you at Elmsford I was enchanted by your youth and freshness, your candour and your quite remarkable talent. But you were about to throw yourself away upon a most uninteresting young man who had no appreciation of your potentialities either as an actress or a woman. I wanted to transplant you into my world, and I hoped, eventually into my arms. I may be shopsoiled and blasé, but I could rejuvenate myself in your youth and in return I would give you stardom. But I was selfish and wrong. I broke up your romance, and what I offered you you didn't want. I should have left you where I found you and not interfered in your life.'

'But you did interfere,' she said softly, 'and it's up to you to make amends.'

'In any way I can.' Their eyes met, in hers was the expression of her love and longing, in his a blue flame. 'If you're prepared to take me,' he said uncertainly, 'a man, I hope, no worse than other men, but on the wrong side of thirty, all that I have is yours, including my heart.'

'That's all I've wanted, all I ever wanted,' she whispered.

He pushed back the chair and dropped on his knees beside her, encircling her with his arm.

'Then what can I give you, darling, since you don't want a career?'

'A home, and children, and your love. All the star-dust in the theatrical firmament can't compensate for lack of those.'

'My dear child, my sweet unsophisticated unexacting child, those you shall have in full measure.'

She wreathed her arms about his neck. 'You do really love me, Philip? You haven't said it.'

'I've been saying it for the past fifteen minutes. I adore you.'

'I can hardly believe this is true. I've wanted you so much ... and I thought my accident would part us for ever.'

'Which brings me back to where I came in. How dare you harbour such a wicked thought? But now I've got you,' his arms tightened and he drew her close against his chest, 'and I'll never let you go, I'll make you pay forfeit for all your doubts of me.'

'I always knew you were a bully...' She got no further, for his mouth came down on hers and neither of them said anything more for a long time.

When Mrs. Brent came in she found them in each other's arms.

'Philip, I thought you were in the States,' she gasped, as he sprang hastily to his feet.

'I was, but as my fiancée was trying to jilt me I had to race back to prevent her.'

Rosamund beamed at the ecstatic girl.

'What did I tell you?'

'Isn't there a house for sale a little further along this road?' Philip asked.

'I believe so. Are you interested?'

'Very. You see, Averil has been cast for a new role, wife and mother, and I need a proper setting for her.' He smiled down at Averil. 'You'll still be my leading lady,' he told her.

Dear Reader,

We at Mills & Boon are only too well aware of the burden of price increases that everyone is having to bear in the present economic situation. So we are constantly looking for new ways to make economies in the production of our books which can help us to maintain our present prices.

Nevertheless we are faced with ever-increasing costs of printing, paper and handling.

In order to avoid passing on the latest round of increases to you, the reader, we have decided to use a slightly thinner paper for our romances, beginning with the April titles. This will make only a small difference to the thickness of each paperback; there will, of course, still be a full 192 pages of romance in each book.

This small change will enable us to keep the price of our paperback romances to 30p and we hope it will help you to enjoy more of the romance reading you know you can rely on.

Yours sincerely,

MILLS & BOON

May Paperbacks

DARK PURSUER
by Jane Donnelly
Nothing was allowed to stand in Connor Lammas's way—
and when his young brother Andrew fell in love with Kate
Howard, Connor was determined to break up the affair.
Kate hadn't wanted to marry Andrew in any case, but now,
in the face of this interference, she decided to dig in her
heels . . .

VALLEY DEEP, MOUNTAIN HIGH
by Anne Mather
Andrea Connolly was convinced that Axel von Mahlstrom
was a fortune-hunter, and she thought out an effective way
of teaching him a lesson. Unfortunately Axel turned the
tables on her in an unexpected and decidedly disturbing
manner . . .

MY LADY DISDAIN
by Elizabeth Ashton
Jacqueline had always loved Gino, and when he asked her
to marry him she gladly accepted—although she knew he
wasn't marrying her for love but because he wanted a
competent helpmeet. Then her glamorous sister came along
and announced that she and Gino were in love. Should
Jac let him go—or should she stick to her rights as his
fiancée?

WIFE MADE TO MEASURE
by Ruth Clemence
Jocelyn had been more or less bullied into marrying Simon
Wadebridge, although she had never been in any doubt
about her feelings for him. It was Simon's feelings for her
that she was unsure about—and all the other beautiful girls
in his life . . .

THE CHILD OF JUDAS
by Violet Winspear
When her cousin Penela jilted the Greek tycoon Lion
Mavrakis, Fenny took her place at the wedding and married
him under false pretences. But when Lion had got over his
first, furious anger, he agreed to keep her as his wife—on
one condition . . .

30p net each

Available May 1976

May Paperbacks *continued*

CLOUDED WATERS
by Sue Peters

The feud between the Montagues and the Capulets was like a childish squabble compared to the long-standing quarrel between the Dane and the Baird families, and it had already ruined the romance between Marion Dane and Adam Baird. But now fate had brought Marion and Adam together again. Was fate in fact offering them a second chance?

SONG OF THE WAVES
by Anne Hampson

It was while she was on a world cruise that young Wendy Brown met Garth Rivers and soon recognised him as the love of her life. Which was ironical, for what Garth did not know was that Wendy's life was not going to last much longer ...

UNDER JOINT MANAGEMENT
by Mary Burchell

Anne knew she was taking a risk in keeping her fiancé waiting on the interests of her family, but in the circumstances it was a risk that just had to be taken, and luckily Gregory was very understanding. But then Anne began to shoulder her employer's responsibilities too – and very nearly lost her happiness as a result.

NOT BY APPOINTMENT
by Essie Summers

Jocelyn, running away from a love that could not be, was thankful to find a job looking after two orphaned children and housekeeping for their uncle. Perhaps it would compensate for the family life that would now never be hers. But then her peace of mind was shattered yet again by the malice of a jealous woman ...

RIDE A BLACK HORSE
by Margaret Pargeter

The advertisement for a Girl Friday seemed just the job Jane was looking for – the chance to work in the country and train for a riding school of her own. The owner, Karl Grierson, was *not* quite what Jane had been looking for, though!

30p net each

Available May 1976

Also available next month, eight titles in our Doctor – Nurse series!

Available April 1976

35p net each

Free! Your copy of the Mills & Boon Catalogue –'Happy Reading'

If you enjoyed reading this Mills & Boon romance and would like to obtain details of other Mills & Boon romances which are available, or if you're having difficulty in getting your ten monthly Mills & Boon romances from your local bookshop, why not drop us a line and you will receive, by return and post free, the Mills & Boon catalogue— 'Happy Reading'.

Not only does it list nearly 400 Mills & Boon romances, but it also features details of all future publications and special offers.

For those of you who can't wait to receive our catalogue we have listed over the page a selection of current titles. This list may include titles you have missed or had difficulty in obtaining from your usual stockist. Just tick your selection, fill in the coupon below and send the whole page to us with your remittance including postage and packing. We will despatch your order to you by return!

MILLS & BOON READER SERVICE, P.O. BOX 236, 14 Sanderstead Road, South Croydon, Surrey CR2 0YG, England.

Please send me the Free Mills & Boon catalogue ☐

Please send me the titles ticked ☐

I enclose £..................(No C.O.D.) Please add 5p per book— standard charge of 25p per order when you order five or more paperbacks. (15p per paperback if you live outside the UK).

Name ....

Address ....

City/Town ....

County/Country...................Postal/Zip Code.......................

*Will S. African & Rhodesian readers please write to:—

      P.O. BOX 11190
      JOHANNESBURG, 2000
      S. AFRICA

NEW TITLES ONLY are available from this address.

MB4/76

Your Mills & Boon Selection!

☐ 998
DANGEROUS RHAPSODY
Anne Mather

☐ 1004
MOONRISE OVER THE
MOUNTAINS
Lilian Peake

☐ 1010
AFFAIR IN VENICE
Rachael Lindsay

☐ 1016
MISS NOBODY FROM
NOWHERE
Elizabeth Ashton

☐ 1018
THE CORNISH HEARTH
Isobel Chace

☐ 1019
PALE DAWN, DARK
SUNSET
Anne Mather

☐ 1020
THE TENDER NIGHT
Lilian Peake

☐ 1021
INNOCENT DECEPTION
Rachel Lindsay

☐ 1022
BOSS MAN FROM OGALLALA
Janet Dailey

☐ 1023
THE SPANISH INHERITANCE
Elizabeth Hunter

☐ 1024
STORM FLOWER
Margaret Way

☐ 1025
THE CRUISER IN THE BAY
Katrina Britt

☐ 1026
DARK VENETIAN
Anne Mather

☐ 1027
BELOVED ENEMIES
Pamela Kent

☐ 1028
ROSE OF THE DESERT
Roumelia Lane

☐ 1029
AUTUMN WEDDING
Anita Charles

☐ 1030
THE RELUCTANT LANDLORD
Sara Seale

☐ 1031
BLOW HOT, BLOW COLD
Betty Neels

☐ 1032
DANGEROUS LOVER
Jane Beaufort

☐ 1033
A LETTER FOR DON
Mary Burchell

☐ 1034
HEART'S EASE
Sherry Standen

☐ 1035
THE FIRE AND THE FURY
Rebecca Stratton

☐ 1036
THE PLAYER KING
Elizabeth Ashton

☐ 1037
ENCHANTMENT IN BLUE
Flora Kidd

All priced at 25p. Please tick your selection and use the
handy order form supplied overleaf.